"Thank you. I really don't know what I would've done—or where I'd be now—if you hadn't appeared."

He knew where she'd be about now—sitting under some hot light, probably tied up and getting interrogated by some very bad people. He would never allow that to happen to her.

He'd been too late to protect her friend, but not too late to protect Sophia. Now that he'd met the woman with the sad childhood and the hard shell, he'd do anything to keep her safe.

He'd never kept anything from his superiors before, but he just might want to conceal his crazy attraction for Sophia. They didn't need to know, even though he wouldn't let his emotions get the better of him.

That had happened only once.

LOCKED, LOADED AND SEALED

CAROL ERICSON

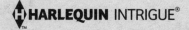

HARLEQUIN INTRIGUE®

For all the military wives who keep it together

Recycling programs
for this product may
not exist in your area.

ISBN-13: 978-0-373-75669-8

Locked, Loaded and SEALed

Copyright © 2017 by Carol Ericson

Printed in U.S.A.

HARLEQUIN®
www.Harlequin.com

Carol Ericson is a bestselling, award-winning author of more than forty books. She has an eerie fascination for true-crime stories, a love of film noir and a weakness for reality TV, all of which fuel her imagination to create her own tales of murder, mayhem and mystery. To find out more about Carol and her current projects, please visit her website at www.carolericson.com, "where romance flirts with danger."

Books by Carol Ericson

Harlequin Intrigue

Red, White and Built

Locked, Loaded and SEALed

Target: Timberline

Single Father Sheriff
Sudden Second Chance
Army Ranger Redemption
In the Arms of the Enemy

Brothers in Arms: Retribution

Under Fire
The Pregnancy Plot
Navy SEAL Spy
Secret Agent Santa

Harlequin Intrigue Noir

Toxic

Visit the Author Profile page at Harlequin.com for more titles.

CAST OF CHARACTERS

Sophia Grant—A physical therapy student with a troubled past, she finally has her life on track until her friend and mentor is murdered and she's thrust into the middle of a terrorist plot. Now she has to overcome her trust issues and place her faith in a sexy navy SEAL sniper who may disappear from her life faster than he appeared.

Austin Foley—A navy SEAL sniper, Austin is sent stateside on a covert mission to protect a former informant. When that informant winds up dead, Austin must shift his focus to protecting the damaged woman who could hold the key to a terrorist attack...and the key to his heart.

Dr. Hamid Fazal—This doctor was whisked out of Pakistan when he provided intel to the United States about a terrorist, but he was tracked down in the United States and murdered, leaving a mystery and a terrified friend.

Peter Patel—Dr. Fazal's friend sets off a chain reaction of events that ends in the death of his friend and a looming catastrophe.

Ginny Faraday—Dr. Fazal's receptionist is an innocent bystander, but even innocent bystanders aren't safe from terrorist plots.

Tyler Cannon—After just one date with Sophia, he already seems ready and willing to be there for her—a little too ready and willing.

Vlad—A sniper for the insurgents during the Gulf War dogged Austin's sniper team at every turn; has his mission morphed into a personal vendetta?

Ariel—The mysterious person on the other end of an email address giving orders to Austin on his mission is willing to circumvent the rules in her quest to bring down Vlad at all costs.

Prologue

A possible target came into view and a bead of sweat rolled down Austin Foley's face and dripped off his chin. It wasn't the mission making him sweat, even though technically the SEALs weren't supposed to be operating in Pakistan; it was the heat rising from his rooftop hideaway, even in the dead of night. The corner of his mouth lifted. He had full confidence in the mission—he always did.

He adjusted his .300 Win Mag slightly to the left, repositioning the target in his crosshairs. The man in his sights had just slipped around the corner of a whitewashed building and stepped around a whirlwind of sand in his path—and his path led to the Jeep parked in front of Dr. Hamid Fazal's house.

"I have eyes on a suspected target. How's it looking, Grayson?"

Chip Grayson, his spotter, sucked in a breath.

"It's that guy who just came around the corner, right?"

"That's our man, and he's heading for the Jeep and Fazal's house. Is the doctor out yet?"

"Not yet. Do you see a weapon?"

"Nope, but I don't see his hands."

"Movement at the front door. Whaddya got, Foley? Do or die time?"

Austin let out a measured breath, the man in the crosshairs his whole world, the man's movements determining Austin's next step and the target's own fate. The suspect turned his head to the side once. Austin blinked. Another drop of sweat plopped to the gravel on the rooftop.

"Fazal's at the door, outside, weapons up."

"The rescue team can't see our guy yet, which means nobody has a clear shot."

"Except you."

"Got that right."

"Are you gonna take it?"

"Patience, my man. He could be a friend coming to say goodbye to Fazal."

"Except nobody's supposed to know he's leaving, especially not in the company of a navy SEAL team."

The man hunched forward suddenly and Austin's finger tightened on the trigger, the action an extension of his brain. The suspect couldn't have a gun. He wouldn't be ducking if he wanted to shoot.

The target pulled his hand from a pocket, clutching something dark and pear-shaped. Austin's jaw tensed as he recognized the object. The man reached for the grenade with his other hand.

Austin took the shot. "Got him."

The man jerked and fell, the grenade dropping from his hand and rolling away from his body.

Grayson got on the radio to the team now assisting Dr. Fazal into the Jeep. After acknowledging Grayson's communication, one of the SEALs broke away and approached the dead man on the street.

A movement on top of a building across the way caught Austin's attention. With his scope, he zeroed in on the sniper raising his rifle and aiming at the SEAL in the street.

Austin took him out…and the fight was on.

Chapter One

Sixteen months later

The soles of Sophia's sneakers squeaked on the slick cement floor of the parking structure. She hit the key fob and her trunk popped open. As she swung her bag into the car, it fell on its side, scattering the contents across the carpeted trunk.

She huffed out a breath and hunched over to collect her junk—a hastily wrapped leftover sandwich from lunch, a dog-eared paperback… and Dr. Fazal's files.

"Damn." She must've swept them up by mistake in her rush to leave the office. She checked the time on her cell phone clutched in her hand, and grimaced. She'd planned to leave work a little early so she could get ready for her date tonight, but Dr. Fazal had wanted her to look up something for him and one thing had led to another, which it usually did with Hamid, including a stop at the pharmacy on her way out. Now she had to return these files to him since he was burning the midnight oil and might need them.

She hadn't disappointed her mentor's faith in her yet and didn't plan on starting now. His belief in her these past months had been the highlight of her year—hell, the highlight of her sorry life.

She grabbed the folders, shoved the rest of the stuff back into the canvas bag and slammed the trunk shut. As she turned with the folders pressed to her chest, a car squealed around the corner from the parking level above hers.

She jumped back, coughing on the exhaust the old beater left in its wake. The car had sped past her and was already too far down the aisle for its driver to benefit from a choice hand gesture from her, so she just shook her head.

Grinning, she shoved that hand into the pocket of her sweater. Dr. Fazal had been helping her curb her temper, too. In fact, the doctor had been like the father she'd never had. So, she had no problem going back up to the office to return his files—even if it did make her late for her date.

She hadn't been having much luck with the guys from that internet dating site anyway, although she had high hopes for Tyler.

The elevator settled on her floor, and she stood to the side as the doors opened in case anyone was coming out, not that she expected people hanging around the office building at this late hour. Dr. Fazal stayed late most nights.

Due to the emptiness of the building, the elevator car sped upward without stopping once. Sophia got off on the fourth floor and almost tripped over Norm's bucket.

Two doors down from the elevator, Norm looked up from his mop. "Sorry, Sophia. I thought you just left."

"I left a while ago, but I had to make a stop at the pharmacy downstairs and then got all the way to my car before I realized I forgot something. I'm assuming Dr. Fazal is still here."

"I just got up to this floor. Heard someone on the stairs a little while ago, and thought it was you. Maybe it was the doc." He returned to his bucket and dredged the mop in the soapy water. "Make sure you walk where it's dry."

"I will." She jingled her office keys in her hand as she made a wide berth around the wet linoleum.

Maybe Dr. Fazal left early tonight, and since he didn't call her about the files, he hadn't missed them. He had seemed distracted all day, for a few days actually, so maybe he'd decided to call it quits.

She strode to the last office on the left, where Dr. Fazal had his orthopedic practice. Leaning into the door, she tried the handle first. He'd locked up since she left.

"Dr. Fazal?" She tapped on the heavy door. Then she inserted her key and pushed it open.

He'd turned off the lights in the reception area, but a glow beyond the front desk area gave her hope. "Hello? I'm back."

She ducked beside a table where someone had fanned out all the magazines from the rack and stacked them together. Ginny from the front desk usually straightened up the reception area on her way out of the office. Sophia dropped the magazines into different slots on the wall rack and opened the door that led to the offices in the back.

The quiet suddenly unnerved her. Hamid must've gone home. She stepped through the door and the toe of her shoe kicked something on the floor. She dropped her gaze and her eyebrows collided over her nose as she nudged the stapler with her foot. Licking her lips, she peered around the corner to the front desk area where Ginny ruled the roost during the day.

Her heart slammed against her chest as she jumped back from the chaos that marred Ginny's typically orderly work area. Someone had whipped open all the drawers, and the contents of those drawers had spilled over onto the floor. The overhead bins yawned open, discharging their contents in a humble-jumble mess.

The hair on the back of her neck quivered, and she twisted her head over her shoulder, almost giving herself whiplash. Were the thieves still here? If they were looking for drugs, they could've targeted a better office.

Swallowing hard, she took one step toward Dr. Fazal's office and the exam rooms and paused with her head cocked to one side. Silence greeted her. They'd either left already or had heard her come in and were lying in wait, ready to pounce.

Her gaze darted to the front door of the office, which had closed behind her. Her street sense told her the thieves had left the scene of the crime. Her street sense was also sending a shiver up her spine.

She crept down the short hallway, trailing her fingers along the wall. She poked her head into exam room one, her jaw hardening. The intruders had rifled through this room, too... and the next.

She continued her stealthy approach to Dr. Fazal's office. He'd be devastated by the violence perpetrated against his practice. He'd come here to get away from the violence of his homeland.

Holding her breath, she walked into his office. She released the breath with a sputter. Someone had ransacked the room. Papers were strewn all over, sofa cushions were pulled out and hastily stuffed back in place and the drawers of the credenza behind Dr. Fazal's big desk stood open and half-empty.

These people must be some stupid junkies to think they were going to find drugs in here— but then weren't all junkies stupid? A heavy smell in the air made her shudder and close her eyes. Reaching for the phone, she stepped around his desk.

She froze. Then she dropped to her knees beside Dr. Fazal crumpled on the carpet next to his chair.

"Dr. Fazal! Hamid!" She curled her arm under his neck to raise his head and blood soaked the sleeve of her sweater. Blood—her subconscious had recognized the smell. One side of Hamid's head had been blown away. She choked out a sob and her throat burned.

The smell of gunpowder permeated the air. Why hadn't she noticed it before? She sat back on her heels and another shock jolted her body—a gun lay next to Dr. Fazal's hand.

"No, no, no." She shook her head. He never

would've taken his own life. Why would he mess up his office first?

She closed her eyes and dragged in a long breath. She didn't like the police, didn't trust the police, but right now she needed the police.

THE BOSTON PD COP, Officer Bailey, scratched his chin with the end of his pencil. "It looks like suicide, ma'am. There's gunpowder residue on the doctor's hand, the shot to the temple looks like it was done at close range."

"And the condition of the office?" Sophia brushed the hair out of her face with the back of her hand. "He ransacked his own office, ran back in here and shot himself because he couldn't find a pencil? That's ridiculous. And I already told the detective that his computer's missing."

"Had you noticed a change in his demeanor lately? Depressed?"

"He was…" She pressed her lips together. She didn't want to betray Dr. Fazal, but she didn't want to withhold any information that might help the investigation into his murder—because this *was* a murder. "He'd been agitated the past few days, distracted."

"Was anyone hanging around the office? Disgruntled patients? Problems with the wife?"

"Dr. Fazal was a widower. I already told the detectives."

"You have my card, Ms. Grant. The detectives on the case will have more questions for you later." He circled his finger around the reception area where he'd been questioning her. The coroner hadn't removed Dr. Fazal's body from the office yet. "We'll finish up here and barricade it as a crime scene. Are you expecting patients tomorrow?"

"It's Saturday. No. But I'll call Ginny Faraday, our receptionist, to let her know what happened. She can start calling our patients."

The cop tapped his notebook. "That's the name and number you gave me earlier?"

"That's right." She hugged the framed picture she'd taken off the floor next to Dr. Fazal's body.

Officer Bailey noticed the gesture and pointed to the picture. "What's that?"

She turned it around to face him. "I-it's a picture of Dr. Fazal congratulating me on an award I won last year."

"Was it in his office?"

"On the floor. He must've knocked it over when he fell." She pressed it to her chest again as one tear rolled down her cheek.

"Sorry for your loss, ma'am. You can take that with you."

Bailey asked her a few more questions, double-checked her contact info and asked her if she wanted an escort to her car.

"I do, thanks." The cops might think Dr. Fazal had committed suicide, but she knew his killers were on the loose out there somewhere.

Bailey called over another officer on the scene. "Nolan, can you walk Ms. Grant down to her car in the parking structure?"

"Absolutely. Lead the way."

Sophia took one last look at the office where she'd spent just about the happiest year of her life and sucked in her trembling bottom lip. Dr. Fazal hadn't killed himself. He wouldn't have left her like that—not like everyone else had.

When Officer Nolan touched her back, she jumped and then barreled out the office door. A detective was questioning Norm by the elevator.

Sophia stabbed the call button and then turned to Norm. "Did you tell the detective that you heard someone on the stairwell right before I came back, Norm?"

"I sure did, Sophia."

"They think it was suicide." She snorted. "No way. You should've seen the office."

"D-do you think that was the doc's killer on the stairs?" Norm's eyes bugged out.

The detective questioning Norm raised his

eyebrows at Officer Nolan. "I'd like to question the witness in private."

"Sure, sure." Nolan's face turned red up to his hairline and he prodded Sophia into the elevator when the doors opened.

When she got inside, she slumped against the wall, folding her arms over the framed picture. "I just wanted to make sure Norm told the detective about hearing someone on the stairwell. That could've been the killer."

"You're convinced Dr. Fazal didn't kill himself?"

"He wouldn't do that."

To me, the voice inside her head screamed. *He wouldn't do that to me.*

She lifted her shoulders and dropped them. "Besides, why would he search his own office like that?"

"Maybe he was looking for something, couldn't find it and decided to end it all. Did you know he kept a gun in his office?"

"Who said it was his gun? Maybe the killers shot him in the head and planted the gun in his hand."

"I guess we'll know more when the homicide detectives look into everything and we get the ballistics report and the autopsy."

The elevator reached level two of the parking garage and the doors opened on an empty aisle.

Sophia grabbed the officer's arm. "Wait a minute. When I was returning to the office, a car came careening around the corner, tires screeching and everything. Do you think it might be connected?"

"What kind of car? Did you get a look at the driver?"

"It was an old car, beat-up, midsize and dark. I didn't see who was driving, but can you tell the detective?"

"I'll tell him and you can tell him yourself when you talk to him again. This lot is straight in-and-out, right? No attendant?"

"If you're a visitor, you take a ticket on your way in and pay at a machine before you leave. There should be some record around that time." She slipped the photo into her purse.

"I'll pass it on. This your car?"

It was the only car left in the aisle, maybe on the entire level.

"This is it. Thanks." She hit the key fob, and the officer waited until she got into the car. She waved at him in her rearview mirror as he stepped back into the elevator.

Then she broke down.

Her messy cry lasted a good five minutes. When she got it all out, she bent forward and reached into her glove compartment for some tissues.

As she straightened up, she heard a whisper of movement behind her. Her eyes flew to the rearview mirror and she met the steady gaze of a man in her backseat.

Chapter Two

Austin held his breath. He had to play this right or this emotionally overwrought woman just might go ballistic on him. And he'd deserve it.

He held up both hands. "I'm not here to hurt you. I'm a friend of Dr. Fazal's, and I think I know what happened to him."

One of her hands was gripping the steering wheel and the other was covering the center where the horn was located. If she drew attention to them, to him, it would be all over.

Her breath came out in short spurts and her gaze never left his in the mirror. "Do you have a gun on me?"

He could tell her he did and she'd probably do whatever he asked, but he didn't want to frighten her any more than he had—any more than she had been by tonight's events.

"I don't have a gun on you. You can lay on

that horn and I'll hightail it out of your car, out of your life, but you may never know what happened to Hamid… And your own life may be in danger."

Her dark eyes, beautiful even with makeup smudged all around them, narrowed—not exactly the reaction he'd expected.

She blew her nose with the tissue and tossed it on the floor of the car. Turning slightly in the driver's seat, she asked, "If you know so much, how come you're not up there right now talking to the Boston PD?"

"For the same reason I didn't come and knock on your front door or give you a call. I'm trying to keep a low profile—for reasons I may not be able to tell you."

"Because you killed him?"

"I didn't kill him, and I won't harm you."

"How do I know that?"

"You're alive, aren't you?" He relaxed in the backseat, his hands on his knees in full view. "You already know I'm no threat to you. You sense it. In fact, you're a street-savvy woman, aren't you, Sophia Grant?"

She spun around to face him. "Who the hell are you? How do you know me? Dr. Fazal?"

He splayed his fingers in front of him. "I'm going to reach into my front pocket."

Nodding, she curled her hands into fists as if ready to take him on.

He slipped his military ID from his pocket and held it in front of her face. "That's me. I'm US military, and I'm on an assignment."

She squinted at the laminated card and shifted her eyes to compare his face to the picture on the ID.

He asked, "Can we go somewhere and talk? You might feel more comfortable in a public place."

"I might feel more comfortable if you sit in the front seat where I can see your hands."

He held up his hands again, pinching his ID between his fingers. "They're right here. I'd rather stay in the back for now. I don't want to be seen in your car in case..."

"In case someone's watching me, following me?" She started the car's engine. "Why would someone be interested in me?"

Why *wouldn't* they be? Austin dragged his gaze from her luscious lips and met her eyes. "Because you worked with Dr. Fazal."

"It wasn't suicide. He didn't kill himself." Her chin jutted forward as if daring him to disagree with her.

"He may have killed himself, but only because he had no choice. The men after him would've killed him anyway—and probably after hours or days of torture."

She gasped and covered her mouth with one hand.

A twinge of guilt needled his belly. He'd gone too far. Just because she hadn't screamed and hit the horn or fainted didn't mean she had a hard shell impervious to pain.

"I'm sorry, and you're right. Dr. Fazal was not suicidal, but I would like a better idea of what was going on with him. Can you help me out?"

"I knew it." She smacked the steering wheel. "Those idiots were trying to tell me he killed himself when the office had obviously been searched."

"Searched?" His pulse sped up. "Was anything taken?"

"Just his computer as far as I could tell. The cops had me look around, but I was too rattled to see straight." She put the car in Reverse and backed out of the space. "I know a place in Cambridge, not too far from here—dark, not too crowded, but crowded enough so that we won't be noticed."

"Sounds good." He ducked down and lay across the backseat. "I'm going to stay down. I want you to check your mirrors when you drive out of the parking structure to make sure you're not being followed. Keep an eye out. Slow down and let cars pass you, take a few turns if you think someone's tailing you."

"You're not making me feel any better."

"You'll be safe—with me." The same couldn't be said for Dr. Fazal, and Austin felt the failure of showing up too late to protect him gnaw at his gut.

The tires squealed and the car bounced as she pulled out of the parking structure. Austin's forehead hit the back of the driver's seat. "Did you see someone?"

"All clear so far. Why?"

"You stepped on that gas like you had the devil himself on your tail."

"To get out of that parking structure, you gotta move or you'll be waiting there all night."

Apparently, every intersection she blew through had the same problem as the car sped up, lurched around corners and jerked to a stop every once in a while. If Fazal's killers didn't end him, Sophia's driving would.

"No headlights behind you?"

"Not for any length of time. Don't worry. I got this. I'm no stranger to losing a tail."

"Should that concern me?"

"It should make you happy. We're almost there."

Rubbing his forehead, Austin sat up and

peered out the window. They'd already crossed Longfellow Bridge and were speeding into Cambridge.

A few minutes later, the car crawled along a street lined with bars and restaurants as Sophia searched for a parking space.

He tapped on the window. "There's a public lot with space."

"Are you kidding? I'm not paying twenty-four bucks to park my car."

"I'll spring for the parking. We could be driving around here all night looking for a place."

"Your call, but it's a rip-off." She made an illegal U-turn in the middle of the street and swung into the lot, buzzing down her window.

He pulled a crumpled twenty and a five from his pocket and handed them to her.

The attendant met the car. "That's twenty-four dollars, please."

She gave him the money, and then pinched the one dollar bill he gave her between two fingers and held it over her shoulder. "Here you go."

When they got out of the car, Sophia crossed her arms, gripping her biceps and hunching her shoulders.

"You don't have a jacket? It's cold out here for just a long-sleeved shirt."

"I had a sweater." She slammed the car door and locked it. "It has Dr. Fazal's blood all over it."

"I'm sorry. Take my jacket." He shrugged out of his blue peacoat and draped it over her shoulders, his hands lingering for a few seconds.

She hugged the coat around her body and sniffed. "Thanks."

They joined the Friday night crowd on the sidewalk—students, professors, young professionals, a few tourists. They could fit in with this bunch, even though Sophia still wore a dazed expression on her pale face.

She led him to one of the many bars, crowded but not jammed, a duo at one end singing a folk song.

"We can probably still get a booth, but we'll have to order some bar food."

"That's okay." He tipped his chin toward a booth in the back of the long room that three people had just left. "There's one."

He followed her as she wended her way through the tables scattered along the perimeter of the bar. Her black hair gleamed under the low lights, and he had a sudden urge to reach out and smooth his fingers along the silky strands. He shoved his hands into the pockets of his jeans instead.

A waitress swooped in just as they reached the table. "I'll clear this up for you."

When the waitress finished clearing the glasses from the previous customers, Sophia slid onto the bench seat and he sat down across from her.

Hunching forward, she buried her chin in her hand and the small diamond on the side of her nose sparkled. "Tell me who you are and what the hell is going on."

"My name's Austin Foley, and I'm in the US Navy."

She blinked her lashes, still long and dark even though her mascara had run down her face. "How do you know Dr. Fazal?"

He massaged his temple. How could he explain things to her without compromising classified information?

Of course, the rescue of Dr. Fazal was no longer classified, and if anyone had a right to know about Dr. Fazal's past, Sophia did. Maybe she already knew. All their intel on Fazal and Sophia indicated that the two had grown close.

"What did Fazal tell you about his past before coming to the US?"

Sophia bit her bottom lip as the waitress approached the table. "Now, what can I get you?"

"I'll have a beer—whatever you have on tap."

"Club soda with lime for me."

The waitress left, and Sophia leaned toward him over the table. "I only know that his wife and two daughters died in a terrorist bombing in Islamabad. The US government resettled him here for safety, but then you know that already. You claim to know more than I do, so you'd better start spilling or I'm calling my new best friends at the Boston PD."

Austin squeezed his eyes shut and pinched the bridge of his nose. If he'd thought handling Sophia Grant would be easy, he'd been completely mistaken. She'd probably catch him out in a lie in about two seconds, too. Were there any girls back home like this? If so, he'd never run into one, and given the size of White Bluff, Wyoming, he'd run into all of the women.

"Okay." He ran a hand across the top of his head, his hair still short from active duty. "Dr. Fazal helped out the US military, helped us nail a wanted terrorist hiding in the area. His life wasn't worth much in Islamabad after that, so we hustled him out of Pakistan."

She nodded. "That doesn't surprise me. I figured there was more to his story."

Nothing seemed to surprise this surprising woman. "We settled him in Boston. You know he went to medical school here?"

"Yes." She drummed her fingers on the

table. "Were you one of the guys who helped rescue him?"

"Uh-huh."

The waitress delivered their drinks and Austin held his up. "To Dr. Fazal."

Sophia clinked her glass with his. "To Dr. Fazal."

She took a sip of her drink and laced her fingers around the glass mug. "What were you doing here at the precise moment he got murdered?"

Austin ground his back teeth together and took a bigger swig of beer than he'd intended. He gulped it down. "He'd contacted us a few weeks back, said he was being watched, followed."

"So *that's* why he'd been agitated."

"Was he?"

"For the past several days—distracted, even curt with me, which was unusual."

"After his initial contact, we didn't hear from him again. I guess he thought we could help him, but I was too late." His hand curled into a fist on the table.

"D-do you think that's it? The people he betrayed in Pakistan wanted revenge?"

"That's what it looks like on the surface, but it's hard for me to swallow that they'd go to all this trouble to get to him. The main guy he betrayed is dead. Were his followers that loyal to track Fazal to the US and murder him here? That's taking a huge chance on their part, and how did they even get into the country if they're on a no-fly list?"

"You're asking me? I'm just a physical therapist in training. You're the—" she waved her hand at him "—navy guy. What is a US military man doing operating on domestic soil, anyway?"

"This is strictly under the radar."

"That's the reason for all the cloak-and-dagger stuff? You're lucky I didn't scream bloody murder and run back to tell the cops a man had broken into my car and had been lying in wait for me."

"Some of it's luck."

"Some?" She raised her dark brows as she took a drink from her glass.

He shrugged. "We had a little intel on you. I didn't figure you for the screaming type."

"That's creepy." She swallowed. "The government can just spy on anyone these days. Is that it?"

"I wouldn't call it spying."

"I would." She flipped her black hair over one shoulder. "So, what do you want from me? I can't give you any more information about Dr. Fazal than I gave the police."

"The Boston PD thinks he may have committed suicide. Now I just gave you this other info about Dr. Fazal. Does this change your view of what was going on with him?"

"He never said anything to me about it, but his killers were definitely searching for something in the office."

"That worries me, makes me think this is about more than revenge."

"What could they have been looking for? Dr. Fazal already gave up what he knew about the terrorist in Islamabad, right?"

"Maybe he had more information that he didn't even tell us." He grabbed a plastic menu from the end of the table. "Are you hungry? The waitress didn't make us order anything, but you probably haven't had dinner."

"I'm not hungry." She clapped a hand over her mouth. "My date."

"You had a date tonight?" Of course she did. An attractive, vibrant woman like Sophia Grant wouldn't be sitting at home alone on Friday night.

"I did. I was supposed to meet him downtown."

"Give him a call. Is there still time?"

"I don't have his phone number, and he doesn't

have mine, thank goodness, or he would've been calling me."

"That's a weird date." He drew his brows together. At least this guy wasn't her fiancé or the love of her life if they didn't even have each other's phone numbers.

"It was a date on Spark."

"Spark?"

"Where've you been, Islamabad?" She tapped her cell phone. "It's a dating app."

"Is that safe?"

"Safer than this." She drew a circle in the air above their table.

"Got me there." He shoved the menu aside and finished his beer. "You'll let me know if anything unusual happens, won't you?"

"Yes, but shouldn't I tell the police, too?"

"Of course, but I'd appreciate it if you didn't mention our meeting. I'm not supposed to be here, not supposed to be investigating this."

"My lips are sealed." She dragged her fingertip across the seam of her mouth. "Where should I drop you off?"

"I'm at a hotel downtown, but since you're in the other direction I can catch the T back to the hotel—unless you want to head downtown to meet your Spark date."

"You know where I live?" She pushed her half-full glass away from her. "Forget the date.

It was just our second. He probably figured I got cold feet."

"Does that happen a lot? I mean, with Spark dates."

"Quite common." She reached into her purse and pulled out a wallet.

"I'll get this. I can call it a business meeting."

"Ah, but you're not supposed to be here, remember?"

"Somebody somewhere has to reimburse me." He dropped a ten on the table. "I'll walk you to your car."

"I really don't mind dropping you off." She scooted from the booth, hugging his coat to her chest.

"That's okay, as long as you keep a lookout when you drive home, just like you did on the way over here."

She jerked her head up. "Do you think I might still be in danger?"

"Not if Dr. Fazal's killers found what they were looking for tonight."

"And if they didn't?"

"They might be at his house right now. Hopefully, the police got there first, but Fazal's killers will return. They might return to the office, too, if they got spooked the first time."

"They might've heard Norm—he's the nighttime janitor."

"Are you going back to the office next week?" He held the door of the bar open for her as she huddled inside his coat.

"Just to wrap up business. All of my patients were Dr. Fazal's patients. We worked together and he referred his patients to me after their surgery, so I could rehabilitate them. I'm not sure what's going to happen now, and I'm not sure what's going to happen to Ginny our receptionist and the two nurses who worked with him." A tear escaped from the corner of her eye and she dashed it away.

"You're going to miss him. He was a good man."

"The best."

Austin tipped his head toward the parking lot down the street. "I'll walk you to your car, and you can drop me at the nearest T station."

The attendant manning the parking lot had called it quits for the night and the entrance was chained off. The exit had spikes to make sure nobody sneaked in that way.

Austin put his hand on Sophia's back as they made their way through the cars.

Out of the corner of his eye, he sensed movement and his reflexes jumped into action. He spun around just in time to see the dull glint of a .45 in the moonlight.

Chapter Three

The mysterious stranger walking beside her shoved her to the ground. She thrust out her hands as she fell to her knees, her palms shredding against the asphalt.

Her instincts had failed her. The guy was turning on her, attacking her. She coiled her body into a crouch. She whipped her head to the side, ready to launch herself at his legs—but which legs were his?

Austin had one arm wrapped around another man as they staggered back and forth under a circle of light from the parking lot. Austin had his right arm thrust in the air at a weird angle, grasping the other man's wrist.

Sophia froze as her gaze focused on the gun clutched in the man's hand, pointing at the sky. How long would it be pointing upward?

As she scrambled toward the other side of the car, someone grunted. Gunfire ripped above her head. She flattened her body against the asphalt, the smell of oil invading her nose. The smell of gunpowder replaced it.

"Hey, hey!"

The male voice came from a distance but Sophia didn't dare lift her head.

A rough hand grabbed her arm, and Austin's harsh whisper grated close to her ear. "Are you okay?"

"Yes. What…?"

He practically yanked her to her feet. "Let's go. Now."

"But…"

He snatched the keys still clutched in her hand and herded her into the car from the driver's side, coming in right behind her. She crawled over the console as Austin made it clear he was taking the wheel. He started the car, and she turned her head toward the passenger window.

A dark figure limped away between the remaining cars as a cop came running up the sidewalk, shining his flashlight into the parking lot.

Without turning on the headlights to the car, Austin pulled out of the lot on the other side of the officer's probing flashlight. When he hit the street, he kept his speed slow and steady until he turned the corner. Then he accelerated until he reached the next major thoroughfare when he put on the lights and reduced his speed to the limit.

That's when Sophia realized she was breathing in short spurts. The whole attack had gone down in a manner of seconds and she still couldn't quite believe it had happened—except for her stinging palms…and the gun in the cup holder.

She rubbed her hands together, loosening bits of gravel into her lap. "What the hell just happened?"

"Are you absolutely sure you weren't followed when you left the medical building?"

If she hadn't fully absorbed the terror of the altercation in the parking lot before, it now hit her like a wall of water.

She gripped the edge of the seat, digging her fingernails into the nubbed fabric. "D-do you think that man had something to do with Dr. Fazal's murder?"

"Of course. Could you have been followed?"

"I don't think so." She pressed her fingertips to her temples. "I watched, just like you said."

He made a sharp right turn and her head bumped the glass of the window.

"Sorry." He pulled the car to a stop along a side street near the MIT campus and jumped out.

With her head spinning, she tumbled out of

the car after him. He was already on the ground, scooting backward beneath the car, propelling himself with the heels of his boots—cowboy boots. What kind of navy guy wore cowboy boots?

"What are you doing?" She crossed her arms over her chest, hugging Austin's jacket around her body, noticing for the first time the fresh, masculine scent in its folds.

He swore and rolled out from beneath the car, clutching something in his fist. Hopping to his feet, he uncurled his hand. "They were tracking you already."

Her mouth dropped open as she stared at the black quarter-size device cupped in his palm. "Why? What do they want from me?"

"I don't know." He tipped his hand and the object fell to the pavement, where he crushed it beneath the heel of his boot. "I don't know what they wanted from Fazal. If it was just revenge they were after, they got that. They didn't have to search his office. And why come after you?"

"Come after?" She fell against the back door of the car.

"I'm sorry, Sophia. Let's get you home."

"Home?" She shuffled away from him. "If they already put a tracker on my car, won't they know where I live?"

"Not if they placed the bug at the office." He

kicked the pieces of the tracking device with his toe, scattering them into the gutter.

"Was that man in the parking lot going to shoot me?"

"I don't think so." He cocked his head to one side and scuffed the bristle on his chin with the pad of his thumb. "He could've taken the shot from farther away. When I saw the gun out of the corner of my eye, the guy didn't have it raised and ready to shoot."

"I suppose that's something to be thankful for."

"He could've wanted info from you."

"But he wasn't expecting you—or at least wasn't expecting my date to be a trained...whatever you are." She waved her hand up and down his body.

"SEAL." He rubbed his hands on the thighs of his jeans. "I'm a navy SEAL."

She narrowed her eyes. "You're a long way from foreign soil where you usually do your thing, aren't you?"

"I thought I explained to you that's why I can't come in contact with the police. It's—" he shrugged "—unorthodox for us to operate stateside."

"Unorthodox or illegal?"

"Depends on who you're asking."

She jerked her thumb over her shoulder. "And

that's why we sneaked away under the cover of darkness and extinguished our headlights back there when the cop showed up?"

"I don't want to have to explain anything. That's not my mission."

"This is a mission?"

"Did you think I was just dropping in on my old friend Dr. Fazal?"

Her nose stung with tears and she squeezed her eyes shut. "He was my friend...and so much more."

He dropped his hand where it lay like a weight on her shoulder. "Do you want me to take you home?"

"Will I be safe there?"

"I'm staying with you—for now."

She studied his strong, handsome face, and the question echoed in her head. *Will I be safe there?*

He blinked. "I'll keep watch over you."

Sighing, she hoisted herself off the car. "I suppose I don't have much choice. I have to go home at some point, might as well be now."

When they got back into the car, Austin turned to her. "You can call the Boston PD right now and let them know you feel threatened—that you think you're being followed. They might step up patrols around your house."

She chewed her bottom lip and traced the

scratches on her palm. Have this navy SEAL, who'd already taken out a guy with a gun, watching over her or the Boston PD, who'd made her life a living hell when she was a teen—easy choice.

"Let's see how it goes before I call in the big guns."

Austin started the car. "Where to? I know you live in Jamaica Plain, but I don't know how to get there without a GPS."

"Back across the bridge. I'll be the GPS." She glanced over her shoulder. "Should I look out for a tail?"

"I think I solved the problem, but it's not a bad idea."

She called out directions as she shifted her attention between the side mirror and the mirror on the visor, watching for headlights and suspicious cars.

Her life growing up had hardly been rainbows and unicorns, but it had just shifted into a strange kind of nightmare that didn't quite seem real. And the man next to her? The most unreal part of it all. He'd literally popped up in the backseat of her car, spouting crazy theories and scaring the spit out of her.

She slid a gaze at his profile. Pretty much everything that had happened tonight, except for Dr. Fazal's murder, had originated with this man.

Yes, she'd seen the stranger with the gun, but had never seen that gun pointed at her. Maybe he was a cop trying to rescue her from Austin. Of course, he had run away, too.

The tracking device on her car? That could've been anything. What did she know about tracking devices?

If Austin had never appeared in her rearview mirror, would she be home snug in her bed, oblivious of gun-wielding assailants and bugged cars? She scooted closer to the door and leaned her head against the cool glass of the window.

With or without Austin, she still couldn't escape the reality of Dr. Fazal's death. He'd seen so much in his life but had gotten to a place where he could appreciate the simple pleasures…and he'd been teaching her to do the same.

A sob escaped her lips and fogged the glass of the window.

Austin touched her knee. "Are you thinking about Dr. Fazal? He was a good man—honorable, courageous. We were both lucky to have known him."

The sincere tone of Austin's voice washed over her like a soothing balm, and a tear welled up in one eye. Only Dr. Fazal had been able to make her cry. Now if she let herself go, she'd never stop—and she already knew tears did nothing but signal your weakness to the world.

She clenched her teeth and dragged in a breath through her nose. Rubbing the condensation from the window with her fist, she said, "He was a great guy…and I'm going to have to find another job."

She could feel Austin's gaze boring into her, and then he removed his hand from her knee.

She tossed back her hair. Let him think she was a cold bitch. She'd opened herself to Dr. Fazal and he'd left her…just like everyone else had. Not that it was his fault. He never would've abandoned her.

"Next?"

"What?"

"Right or left?"

She jerked her head up. She hadn't even been checking the mirrors. She bolted up and grabbed the visor.

"It's okay. I've been watching."

"Left."

She trapped her cold hands between her knees and took a deep breath. "Why are you here? You were responsible for getting Dr. Fazal out of Pakistan and, what? You kept tabs on him?"

"Me personally? No." He cranked up the heat in the car. "US intelligence? Yes."

"CIA?"

"Sort of. There are intelligence organizations under the umbrella of the CIA that are deep undercover."

"You work for one of these organizations?"

"I'm a United States Navy SEAL."

"But one of these organizations contacted you, right?"

He nodded once.

She hunched forward, stretching her fingers out toward the warm air seeping from the vent. "Are you revealing too much? You're not going to have to kill me now, are you?"

He raised one eyebrow without cracking a smile at her clichéd joke. "You're in the middle of this. You deserve to know."

"Am I? In the middle of this?"

"Fazal's killers put a tracking device on your car and tried to pull a gun on you. What do you think?"

The warm air blowing from the vent couldn't melt the chill stealing across her body. She snuggled into Austin's jacket and the comforting scent from its folds. "I think I'm in the middle of it. These intelligence agencies must've known Dr. Fazal was in danger since you showed up at the precise time he was murdered."

Austin's hands tightened on the steering wheel. "I failed him."

"Had you been watching him?"

"I just got to Boston this morning. I read the file on the plane. I read about you, your job, your car, even your address."

Checking the mirrors again, she slumped in her seat. "So much for privacy."

Her paranoia about authority hadn't been misplaced all those years. They really *were* out to get her. Did Austin also know about her messed-up past?

He snorted. "There is no privacy."

"You knew all that, but you hadn't seen Dr. Fazal yet?"

"I showed up at the office building minutes after the first responders did. Then I located your car in the parking structure and waited for you."

"You were supposed to protect Dr. Fazal?"

"I was." His jaw formed a hard line.

"Those intelligence organizations don't sound very intelligent. They should've called you in sooner. You could've done something then."

She didn't know why she wanted to make this supremely confident man feel better. Maybe it was the clenched jaw showing that he was human after all. He clearly felt as if he'd failed Dr. Fazal—and she knew all too well what failure felt like.

"Maybe. Or maybe his killers made their

move today because they knew we were on to them."

"Who are *they*? Who killed Dr. Fazal?" She tapped on the window. "Turn right."

"It depends on the motive. If it was revenge for working with us to capture the terrorist we'd been tracking, then we know it's that terrorist group, but if it's something else…" He shrugged.

"What else could it be?"

"You tell me. Why'd his killers search his office? Why'd they come after you?"

She turned to him, her mouth gaping open. "You expect me to know that?"

"You worked with him. You were close to him. He treated you like a daughter. We know that."

Her throat felt heavy and she cleared it. "He told me very little about his life before. He always emphasized looking forward."

"You said you noticed something different about him in the past few weeks. Was he nervous? Jumpy?"

"Yes." They'd had a dinner planned and he'd cancelled it. He never canceled plans with her because he knew how much stability meant to her.

"How so?"

"He was secretive. He took a few phone calls

behind closed doors. He also saw some mysterious patient. He gave me his file, but he never included the person's information in the regular patient database."

"Is this your street?"

"The apartment building at the end of the block on the right."

"That behavior was unusual for him?"

"It was in retrospect. If he hadn't been murdered today, I probably wouldn't have thought much about it—except for the dinner."

"What dinner?" He pulled the car alongside the curb in front of her apartment building and left the engine running.

Did he expect her to hop out and go up to her apartment by herself while he left her car at the curb and loped off into the night? Hadn't he assured her he'd keep watch tonight? Of course, he owed her nothing.

She coughed into the sleeve of his jacket. "We had dinner at least once a month, and he canceled this month."

"He never canceled before?"

"Never. I mean, I did once or twice, but once Dr. Fazal made plans he kept them."

"If they'd just killed him, that would've been the end of it. But why the search?"

This time she knew it was a rhetorical question, as Austin stared out the window at nothing.

He reached for the ignition. "Should I park here or do you have a parking spot?"

She released a breath. He wasn't ditching her—yet. "If you go up ten feet, there's an entrance to our underground parking garage. I'll direct you to my spot."

They rolled into the garage and she pointed out her parking space, which she'd left what seemed like a lifetime ago but had only been that morning.

"I'll go up with you just to make sure everything's okay, and then I can check your security and monitor the front of your building and watch the elevators."

"A-all night?"

"Whatever it takes."

He said those three words with such conviction, she had a feeling Austin would always do whatever it took.

"Thanks." Was that enough? What did you say to someone who'd just saved your life? She hadn't even thanked him for that. "A-and thanks for saving me from the man with the gun back in Cambridge."

"Of course."

She slipped out of the car and he was beside her in a second. When they got into the elevator, she pushed the button for her floor. "I'm on the third floor."

As they passed the second floor, Austin pulled a gun from his waistband and crowded her to the back of the car. He raised his weapon and the door opened—on her empty floor.

She huffed out a breath, feeling dizzy with relief. "My place is on the left, smack in the middle of the floor."

She held out her hand for her key chain but he shook his head.

When they reached her door, he tucked her behind his body and dangled the keys from one finger. "Which one?"

She tapped her front door key and he inserted it into the deadbolt lock above the door handle and unlocked it. Then he opened the door, and stepped inside, leading with his gun.

"Wait outside the door for a minute."

She held her breath as he stepped inside, continuing to lead with his gun.

He disappeared inside and her heart skipped a beat. "Everything look okay?"

"Just a minute."

His voice sounded muffled, and a picture flashed in her head of Austin going through her closet and personal effects. Gripping the doorjamb, she leaned into her small living room. "Nothing looks out of place in the living room."

Austin emerged from the hallway, his gun

still out but dangling at his side. "I wanted to make sure no one was hiding in the back."

"First time I've ever felt good about my small apartment."

"Nothing's out of place?" His eyes flicked over the sparse room, devoid of personal photos and treasured mementos.

She pulled back her shoulders and marched to the console that housed her TV and a few books and placed the cracked photo of her and Dr. Fazal, which had been stashed in her purse since she'd left the office, on a shelf.

"Everything looks fine in here. Nobody under the bed?"

"Or in the closets or hiding in the tub behind the shower curtain, but only you can determine if anything's messed up."

Again that quick glance around her sterile living room. Could she help it if she traveled light? She'd always had to pick up and go at the drop of a hat, so she kept her possessions at a minimum.

"I'll check the bedroom and bathroom—good thing there's only one of each."

Austin trailed her as she took a few steps down the short hallway and turned into her bathroom. A small row of bottles stood at attention on the right-hand side of the vanity, her electric toothbrush claiming the left. She tugged open the mirrored medicine chest that contained toiletries, no medicine. She didn't believe in drugs.

When she closed the cabinet, she met Austin's green eyes in the mirror. How had she missed those eyes before? Probably because this was the first time she'd seen him in full light. Even the bar in Cambridge had been dark.

"All good."

She pointed to the shower curtain dotted with blue seahorses. "You moved that, right?"

"I swept it aside and back again."

"Next room."

She kept her distance as Austin awkwardly backed out of the bathroom. His presence overwhelmed the small space—overwhelmed her.

He stood aside, flattened against the wall as she brushed past him on her way to the bedroom.

She walked into her room and surveyed the matching bed, nightstand and dresser, and a little smile curled her lips. She'd just bought the matching set two months ago—her very first matching furniture, her very first new furniture.

She passed by the bed and ran her fingertips along the green-patterned bedspread. Then she tripped to a stop as a wave of adrenaline washed through her body and a strangled cry twisted in her throat.

"What's wrong?" Austin placed his hand on the small of her back.

She turned toward him and had the strongest desire to throw herself against his solid chest. Instead she dragged in a long breath and whispered, "Someone was here."

Chapter Four

Austin's gaze dropped to Sophia's trembling bottom lip and he had the strongest desire to take her in his arms and make this all go away for her. But a woman like Sophia—prickly and independent—wouldn't appreciate the gesture. Would she?

"How do you know?" He flicked a lock of her black hair from her eye and she jerked back. He dropped his hand.

"It's the bed. Someone was on my bed."

His gaze skimmed the neatly made bed covered with a green floral bedspread and fluffy pillows stacked against the headboard. "How can you tell?"

"Look at the center of the bed." She tugged his sleeve. "There's an indentation. The pillows are flat...and the smell."

He lifted his nose to the air and sniffed the

faint perfumed odor. He'd figured it had come from a candle or room freshener. It was that faint.

"What is that smell?"

"It's men's cologne. I hate men's cologne." She grabbed one of her decorative pillows and pressed it against her face. "And it's all over this pillow."

He took the pillow from her, dipping his head to the pillowcase covering it. He noticed a spicier, slightly musky scent now and raised his eyebrows at Sophia. She'd make a great detective, but she was perceptive just about her own possessions. The occupant of this apartment could be a monk if he didn't know better. Everything had a place. Fazal's killers couldn't have picked a worse apartment to try to get away with a covert search.

"They were very careful. This guy—" he motioned to the bed "—must've had a temporary lapse or maybe he just got tired after a full day of killing, stalking and searching."

Sophia sucked in a breath and grabbed his sleeve again. "What does this mean? Nobody followed us from Cambridge."

"They already knew where you lived, Sophia. Probably knew all about you, like we did."

"What are they looking for?" Her head cranked back and forth, taking in the bedroom.

"The same thing they were looking for in Fazal's office when they killed him."

"Why do they think I have it?" Her eyes widened even more. "Do you think Ginny, Morgan and Anna could be in danger, too?"

"The receptionist and the nurses? I don't think so. They didn't have the same kind of relationship as you did with Dr. Fazal."

She hunched her shoulders. "I don't know what they think I have or what I can tell them. Dr. Fazal wouldn't confide anything like that in me. Sh-should I just talk to them and tell them that?"

"No!" He took her by the shoulders, his thumbs pressing against the creamy skin above her sweater. "You don't want any contact with these people. Do you think they'll just question you and release you? They'll question you, all right, but it won't be pretty."

She clamped both hands over her mouth, her eyes glassy with unshed tears.

"I'm sorry." This time he did pull her against his chest, wrapping his arms around her. "But that's a really bad idea."

Her body stiffened, and he loosened his grip to allow her an escape. Sophia Grant would always need an escape. She surprised him by leaning into his body, although she kept her arms dangling at her sides.

"What should I do now? They obviously broke into my apartment without any great effort and without anyone seeing them."

"Right this minute?" He took her hands. "You're going to call the police and let them know what happened. The Boston PD has a criminal investigation open in the case of Dr. Fazal's murder, and you're going to let that play out."

"You don't think the cops will ever find his killers, do you?"

"No, but given who the victim was in this case, the FBI will be moving in shortly, anyway."

She broke away from him and swept her arm across the bed. "And what do I tell the cops? I noticed a wrinkle on my bedspread? You believed me because you know who we're dealing with. They'll just think I'm crazy—been there, done that with the cops."

"Your coworker and friend was just murdered today and you found the body. I think the officers will be understanding."

She rolled her eyes. "You don't know the cops like I do. And you won't be here to back me up, will you?"

"No, I can't be here, but you need to report this and get it on record—whether they believe you or not."

She backed away from him and fell across the bed, flapping her arms like she was making a snow angel. "This'll make it a little more believable."

"You could've just contaminated some evidence." He eyed the rumpled covers.

She peered at him through the strands of hair that had fallen across her face when she'd collapsed on the bed. "C'mon, Foley. You and I both know the guys who broke into my place didn't leave any evidence behind—just the smell of some cheap cologne."

His nostrils flared. Did the aftershave he used smell like cheap cologne? Good thing he hadn't shaved this morning.

"Then call the cops and I'll take a walk around the neighborhood. They're going to ask you if anything's missing. Is there? Computer?"

"I take my laptop with me to work, and it's still in the trunk of my car."

"Not a great idea to leave it there." He snapped his fingers. "Why don't you give me your keys so I can go down and get it? You can call the cops in the meantime, and while they're here I'll take a look at your computer—if that's okay."

Hoisting herself up to her elbows, she asked, "Look at my computer? What for?"

"To see if I can find out what Fazal's killers

might be looking for. Maybe you do have something from Hamid and you just don't know it."

"I really don't want anyone going through my computer files."

"I understand." He held up his hands. Not that he didn't already know a lot about her life.

She studied his face as if reading him. Then she bounced up from the bed. "Okay. You can look through my computer, but stick to my emails and a folder on my desktop called Work. Anything Dr. Fazal sent me went into that folder."

"Got it." He followed her into the living room, where she swept her key chain from the table by the front door.

She dangled it in front of him. "I'm going to call the police right now. You don't have to come back up here."

"They might ask to see your keys." He tossed the key chain in the air. "Call them now, report the break-in and make it known you found Dr. Fazal's body today. They'll come out for that. I'll return your keys and hang around until the cops get here, so you don't have to be afraid."

"I won't be afraid. I have a nice little .22 tucked in my closet—not that I'm going to show it to the cops."

His brows shot up. "Did you check to see if it's still there? In fact, you'd better give this place the once-over again to see if anything's been taken. The police are going to ask you, and it'll seem off if you haven't bothered to check."

"I will. Go."

He grabbed the jacket she'd shrugged off earlier and headed back to her car. The trunk lights illuminated her laptop case and a canvas bag, so he grabbed both. When he got back to her apartment, she met him at the door.

"I called the police and they're sending two patrol officers over to take a report."

"Gun still there?"

"The gun and everything else—not that I have anything of value in here—but we both know these so-called thieves were not here to snatch some jewelry and a camera."

"I'll be watching from the twenty-four-hour fast-food place down the block. As soon as they leave, I'll be back." He dumped her keys into her outstretched palm.

As he turned, she grabbed a handful of his jacket. "Where was I between the time I left the crime scene and the time I walked into my apartment and realized someone had been in here?"

"Stay as close to the truth as possible. You stopped for a drink to settle your nerves, but you were nowhere near Cambridge. We don't want them putting you near the shot that was fired and start asking why you ran from the officer there."

"Glad to see I'm not the only one who lies to the police."

Slinging Sophia's laptop case over his shoulder, he made his way to the sidewalk in front of her building. He looked both ways. Did Fazal's killers realize that Sophia had a companion now—one who could take down a man with a gun? They might just have him pegged as a random boyfriend who knew a few moves.

He strode to the next apartment building and ducked behind a wall, away from the glow of the streetlamps. He transferred his weapon from his waistband to the pocket of his jacket and waited.

About fifteen minutes later, a patrol car rolled down the street and stopped in front of Sophia's apartment. Austin waited until the two officers disappeared into the building, and then he loped down the sidewalk toward the orange neon sign boasting all-night burgers.

Pushing through the glass doors, he did a quick survey of the room, his gaze sweeping past the old homeless guy in the corner warming his hands on a Styrofoam cup of coffee and a hipster couple sucking down a couple of milk shakes. He narrowed his eyes at a single man sitting at a table against the wall, clicking away on his laptop.

Must be here for the free Wi-Fi.

Austin approached the counter and nodded to the young woman welcoming him with a big smile and a jaunty hat. He had to give her credit for keeping up the enthusiasm at this time of night.

"Can I get a cup of coffee and an apple pie?"

"Is that for here or to go?" She tapped the computerized register.

"For here, ma'am."

He waited for his snack at the counter, and then took a seat across from the front door where he could keep an eye on it and the man on the laptop.

He pulled Sophia's computer from its case and centered it on the table next to his coffee and prefab pie. As the laptop powered up, he drummed his thumbs on the edge of it and held his breath. He'd forgotten to ask her about a password.

The monitor blinked to life and an array of folders appeared on a backdrop of wildflowers. He recognized the scene as a standard selection from the computer's templates—not that he ever expected Sophia Grant to have a personal photo as her computer's desktop background. Did she even own any personal photos?

He spotted the Work folder and double-clicked on it. The folder contained more folders, some with last names as titles and some with dates.

Only Sophia could tell him if these folders had anything unusual in them. Would Dr. Fazal have put any sensitive information on Sophia's computer if that data could endanger her life? Maybe he'd done so inadvertently.

The folders with the last names were obviously patient files. What had Sophia said about a mysterious patient? Fazal had given her the person's file but hadn't entered the information in their patient database, so maybe it was one of these.

She'd have to show him which one.

Yawning, he popped the lid off his coffee and took a sip. He broke off one corner of his pie to get the slightly burned coffee taste out of his mouth.

The couple with the shakes made a move and exited the restaurant with their heads together. The guy with the laptop followed the pair with his eyes before meeting Austin's gaze for a split second and then returning to his work. Probably idle curiosity—unless he was a private eye spying on them.

Austin took another bite of his warm apple pie, licked the cinnamon goo from his lips and brushed the sugar from his fingers. He closed the Work folder and clicked on the email icon.

Sophia's inbox opened, and a few new messages loaded—all from the same person, someone named Spark or Sparks. He hunched forward and then jerked back when he realized Spark was the online dating site she'd mentioned earlier.

His fingertips buzzed. He wanted to open one of those messages, but she'd realize he'd been snooping. He tracked down the list of messages and saw a few more from Spark—already opened. Didn't he have a right to snoop a little? He was trying to protect this woman.

He double-clicked on one of the messages and immediately felt a sinking sensation in the pit of his stomach as he read some guy's advertisement for himself. He closed the message.

He had no right to delve into Sophia's private business that had occurred before Fazal's murder. He took another bite of his pie. But he'd ask her to go through her new messages and look for anything unusual. She had to be careful now.

He entered Fazal's name in the search field of her inbox and went through those messages, but didn't see anything that raised any red flags. It would be better to do this whole computer exercise with Sophia by his side.

He checked the time in the corner of the computer display and closed out Sophia's mail. The cops had to be done by now. He stowed away the laptop and dumped his trash in the bin.

Calling out a thank-you to the bored fast-food workers, he pushed through the doors and into the cold Boston night air. He shoved his hands into his pockets, curling the fingers of his right hand around the handle of his gun.

When he saw that the patrol car had left, he picked up his pace until he was jogging, his boots scuffing on the sidewalk. He went up through the garage to take a quick look at Sophia's car. Arriving at her apartment door, he tapped once with his knuckle. She had a peephole and he expected her to use it.

She must've been waiting for him because the door swung open immediately. "Well, that was a big waste of time."

"Was it?" He swung the laptop case from his shoulder and put it on the coffee table in front of the sofa. "What did they have to say?"

"A whole lotta nothing."

She'd changed from her dark slacks and sweater into a pair of sweats and a Boston University sweatshirt. She'd pulled her dark hair into a ponytail and must've washed her face, as her dewy skin was devoid of makeup.

"Looks like they left a while ago. I'm sorry. I

should've come back sooner." If he hadn't been prying into her Spark emails...

"They left about ten minutes ago and if they'd had their way, they would've left even sooner."

"Did they believe you?" He pointed to the kitchen. "Can I have some water? That coffee was pretty bad."

"I'll get it." In just a few steps, she reached the kitchen and poured him a glass of water from a dispenser in the fridge. As she handed him the glass, she said, "They didn't say they didn't believe me...but they didn't believe me."

"Even with that messed-up bed."

"I know, right? Imagine what they would've thought about that crease in the bedspread."

"But they knew about Dr. Fazal's murder?"

"That's basically why they came out. They thought I was just being jumpy, but they were okay. Stayed longer than they wanted to or had to." She dipped down and patted her laptop case. "How about you? Did you find anything?"

He felt a warm flush spread through his chest under her dark gaze. *She knew.*

"I think you're going to have to do the investigating. I don't know what those patient files are supposed to look like and if there's anything weird about them." He tapped his chin and as his scruff scratched his fingertips, now he wished he would've shaved after he got off the plane this morning. "I thought about the patient you'd mentioned before—the one Fazal didn't enter in the regular database."

"Yeah, his mysterious patient who didn't need any follow-up exercises."

"Do you remember his name?"

"Peter Patel."

"Patel?"

"Indian, right?"

"A very common Indian name."

"Like Smith or Jones would be in the US."

"Exactly."

"So, if an Indian man…"

"Or Pakistani."

"If he wanted a common name, he might choose Patel."

"The mystery patient could've been a friend of Dr. Fazal's."

"A friend he didn't want to acknowledge for some reason."

"A friend from the past, from Dr. Fazal's homeland, someone who knew what he'd done."

She twisted her ponytail around her hand and screwed up the side of her mouth. "Do you think Patel killed Dr. Fazal?"

"If Peter Patel, or whatever his name is, was Dr. Fazal's enemy, I doubt Fazal would've pretended he was a patient and protected his identity. I'm thinking he was a friend, someone who needed help."

"And that help may have gotten Dr. Fazal murdered—figures he'd think of someone else before himself." She rubbed her nose with the back of her hand.

Austin tipped his head toward the laptop. "Do you want to take a look now or are you ready for bed? It's late."

"I'll look now." She sat on the floor in front of the coffee table and crossed her legs beneath her. "What are you going to be doing tonight while I'm…sleeping?"

"Keeping watch." He sank onto the couch across from Sophia, his knees banging against the coffee table.

"Outside all night?"

"If you don't mind, I thought I'd camp out on your couch. I'm a light sleeper. If anyone tried to break in, I'd know it."

She tapped her keyboard. "Do you think someone might try it?"

"Someone got in here before, and it doesn't seem as if he found what he wanted. He'll try again."

"Are you going to take up permanent residence on my couch?" She peered at him over the laptop lid.

"Sophia, you're going to have to get out of here. It's not safe."

"Are you kidding? Where will I go? How will I afford it?"

"I can take care of all of that. You're a possible source of information for this case—and it's a very important case. We'll keep you safe."

"I've heard that one before." She held up one finger. "Got him. Peter Patel, knee injury."

He hunched forward and she spun the computer to the side so he could see the monitor. An intake form filled the screen—name, address and other vitals.

"Can you print this out?"

"Done." She clicked the screen and a printer across the room buzzed to life. "Are you going to pay Mr. Patel a visit?"

"Since he won't be coming back to the office, yes."

"Can I come?"

"No." He tapped the screen. "Do you see anything out of the ordinary?"

"Other than the fact that this information wasn't entered into our patient database? No." She pushed up and crossed the room to grab the printouts. Then she slid them on the table in front of him. "Anything else you want me to check out?"

"Let's start with Patel."

She kneeled in front of the computer and her fingers flew across the keyboard. "My Spark date from tonight sent me an email. Said he understood if I changed my mind but asked if I wanted to try again."

"No." He grabbed Patel's paperwork and squinted at it as if it were the most fascinating data ever.

Her dark eyes narrowed. "That's rather intrusive considering you and I just met today."

"I don't think it's a good idea to date random strangers—especially now."

"I'd been chatting with this guy long before Dr. Fazal's murder, and we already had one date."

"Even if you weren't a target for terrorists, online dating isn't safe. You can't meet guys the old-fashioned way?"

Doubling over, she banged her head on the coffee table and snorted...or coughed...or maybe that was a laugh. Then she tipped her head back. "Old-fashioned way? You mean bars? I don't do bars, don't drink. Besides, online dating has become one of the most common and popular ways to meet people. Where have you been hiding?"

"Umm, a variety of places around the world—wherever I'm deployed."

"Oh, yeah. I forgot about that." She shut down

her computer and snapped the cover shut. "Trust me. Online dating is the way to go."

"Seems kind of impersonal."

"You got that right." She formed her fingers into the shape of a gun and pointed at him. "I'm going to sleep. I'll get you a blanket and a pillow for the couch. Should I take my .22 to bed with me?"

"That's okay. I'll take care of the firepower."

"You don't trust me? I'm a pretty good shot."

"That's a handy skill to have, but I'll keep watch. You go to bed and think about where you want to move tomorrow."

She put her laptop away and disappeared into the hallway for a minute. She returned with a folded blanket and a pillow from her bed in her arms with a toothbrush in its original package on top.

She tossed the toothbrush to him. "Courtesy of my dentist."

"Floss, too? I'm a flosser."

Tipping her head to one side so that her ponytail swung over her shoulder, she said, "I figured you for a flosser. Top right drawer of my vanity."

"Thanks, Sophia."

She folded her arms, grabbing handfuls of her Boston U sweatshirt at her sides. "No, thank *you*. I really don't know what I would've done—

or where I'd be now—if you hadn't appeared in the backseat of my car after..."

Choked up by emotion or embarrassed by it, she spun around and made a beeline for her bedroom, slamming the door behind her.

He grabbed the toothbrush and took it with him to the bathroom. He knew where she'd be about now—sitting under some hot light, probably tied up and getting interrogated by some very bad people. He would never allow that to happen to her.

After brushing his teeth he settled on the couch and flicked on the TV, his Glock beside him. Being on watch without his Win Mag always felt a little strange, but then everything about this assignment was strange.

He'd been too late to protect Dr. Hamid Fazal, but not too late to protect Sophia Grant. Now that he'd met the woman with the sad childhood and the hard shell, he'd do anything to keep her safe.

He'd never kept anything from his superiors before, but he just might want to conceal his crazy attraction to Sophia. Ariel, the woman he was supposed to be reporting to didn't need to know, even though he'd never allow his emotions to get the better of him.

That had happened only once.

Chapter Five

The next morning, Sophia tiptoed out of her bedroom into the living room, but she needn't have bothered. Austin, sitting on the edge of the couch, the pillow and folded blanket at one end, was clicking away on his cell phone. A flosser and an early riser.

She crossed her arms over the baggy T-shirt she wore to bed to match her equally baggy sweats. For the first time in about ever, she wished she had one of those filmy negligees to slink around in. Maybe she could actually get the man to notice when she walked into a room.

She cleared her throat. "Good morning."

He jerked his head up. "Whoa. Why are you sneaking around?"

"I thought you might be sleeping." She tugged on the hem of her T-shirt. "All quiet last night?"

"Yep." He returned to his phone.

"Coffee?" She strolled into the kitchen and

grabbed the coffeepot. "Do you think the people after me know that you're here?"

He rose from the couch and stretched, his plain white T-shirt straining across an impressive set of muscles. "I think so, but whether or not they know who I am and why I'm here is a different story."

The water from the faucet had spilled over the top of the coffeepot and splashed over her hand while she'd been ogling Austin's physique. She shut off the faucet and tipped the excess water into the sink. "Would they have any reason to believe you'd be here?"

"Me, personally? No." He crossed his arms and leaned against her kitchen table, dwarfing it. "But they might suspect that US Intelligence is onto them, especially after the murder of Fazal. They know there's no way we'd let Fazal's death go unnoticed and uninvestigated."

"Was Dr. Fazal doing any work for the intelligence agencies? I mean currently?"

"Not that I know of, but then, I'm not privy to that kind of information. I protected the doctor once, and was called in on this assignment because he contacted an intelligence officer and because of the chatter."

"What kind of chatter?"

Austin put a finger to his lips. "Top secret.

Do you just drink coffee for breakfast or do you actually have food in that kitchen?"

Holding up her hand, she ticked off each finger. "Bagels, cereal—the healthy kind—eggs."

"If it's okay with you, I'll toast a bagel. Cream cheese?"

"Just butter."

"I can work with that." He circled into the kitchen, immediately making the space feel even more small and cramped than it was.

She pressed her back against the counter, sliding her hands behind her. "Bagels in the breadbox, next to the toaster."

Her phone buzzed on the counter and she checked the display. A knot tightened in her belly. "It's Morgan O'Reilly, one of Dr. Fazal's nurses."

"Aren't you going to answer it?"

"I—I'm not going to say anything about you."

"That's right."

She blew out a breath and answered the call. "Hi, Morgan."

The woman sniffled. "Oh, my God, Sophia. I can't believe it. Was it a robbery? Is that what the cops are calling it? They told me the office was trashed."

"It was, but I don't know if anything was missing. I expect the cops will want Ginny to do an inventory of the drugs."

"We didn't have that many drugs. I could think of a few offices that would have a lot more than us." Morgan blew her nose. "We're going in today, Anna and I. The cops told us we could come in after noon. Do you want to join us? You'd know as much as we would if something was missing."

"Yeah, yeah, if the cops said we could come in." She reached across the kitchen and nudged Austin.

"I think they want us to start picking up the pieces to see what's what."

"I'll definitely be there."

She glanced at Austin, who nodded as he dropped two halves of a bagel into her toaster.

She and Morgan comforted each other with a few more meaningless words, and then she ended the call. "We're all meeting at the office after twelve o'clock."

"Are the police going to be there? Is it still a crime scene?"

"I don't know. Since they gave us a specific time, maybe not." She turned toward the counter and poured the coffee into two mugs. "Were you planning on coming along?"

"I'll go with you, but I'm not going into the office. I don't want to explain myself to the Boston PD. Remember—" he pinched a bagel half between two fingers and tossed it onto a plate "—I'm not supposed to be here."

"Milk? Sugar?"

"Black."

She carried both mugs of coffee to the table and sat down. "Do you have a car?"

"It's at my hotel. I walked to the office."

"Your hotel is downtown?"

"Just a few blocks from Dr. Fazal's office." He sat across from her, putting the plate between them. "Do you want the other half?"

She picked up one half of the bagel and bit into it. The butter ran down her chin and she swiped it away with her fingers. "What's the plan?"

"I'm going to drop you off at the office where you can have a look around with the others. If you see anything out of the ordinary, take a picture for me." He tapped his chin. "More butter."

Her face warm, she jumped up from the table and ripped two pieces of paper towel from the rack. In her sweats and T-shirt with butter dripping off her chin, she must've presented an appealing picture. Not that she'd ever cared what kind of picture she presented before this hot navy SEAL had landed on her couch. Who knew she'd ever be attracted to a military guy, since she usually avoided authority figures like the plague.

When she returned to the table, she waved a paper towel in front of him and he snatched it from her.

She wiped her chin with the other. "Where are you going to be while I'm sifting through the office?"

"I'm going to pick up my laptop at the hotel before I drop you off." He plucked the white T-shirt from his chest with two fingers. "Shower and change, and then I'll find a nice Boston coffeehouse where I'm going to do a little research on Peter Patel."

"Then should we come back here?" Her gaze darted around her small apartment, which had been her first real home.

"Absolutely not. This place is compromised." He swallowed the last bit of his bagel and dragged the paper towel across his mouth. "You can stay at the hotel with me…for now."

She gulped a mouthful of coffee. "How long is this twenty-four-hour protection going to last? I have a life—sort of."

"Until we can figure out who murdered Dr. Fazal, why and what they want with you."

"Couldn't that take years?"

Austin's green eyes flickered. "It's not going to take years, and I know Dr. Fazal would want us to protect you so any life you have can be put on hold for your own safety."

"Maybe this is all some big mistake." She collected the plate and her coffee cup. "It could just be a robbery turned deadly."

"Could be, but I doubt it. Not after the chatter we heard involving Dr. Fazal, not given Fazal's background. I'm sorry, Sophia." He pushed back from the table and took the dishes from her hands, his fingers brushing hers. "Why don't you get ready, pack a bag, take what you'll need for a week or two."

"A week or two?" She raised her eyebrows.

"To be on the safe side."

He kept using that word—*safe*—but she didn't feel safe at all, not when her world had just been turned upside down for the umpteenth time in her life.

"Give me about half an hour, and help yourself to another bagel."

In her bedroom, she grabbed the new pair of jeans she had been planning to wear on her date last night and a red sweater. She slipped from her room to the bathroom and ran the water to warm it up. She dropped her sweats on the floor and then touched the edge of the toothbrush Austin had used last night.

There hadn't been many toothbrushes perched on the edge of the sink like this in her life. When she dated, she tended to keep the guys away from her apartment. It had taken her a long time to have a space just for herself after all the foster care living, and she didn't take it for granted.

Still—she dropped Austin's toothbrush next to hers in a cup—that one looked right.

She showered in a matter of minutes, keeping her hair on top of her head. She dressed in front of the mirror and shook out her hair, the black locks dancing loosely around her shoulders. She ran her hands through the strands, keeping the messy look. She didn't want Austin to think she'd tried too hard with her appearance.

She gathered her sweats and tucked them beneath one arm. Poking her head out of the bathroom door, she called out. "Just give me another fifteen minutes to pack up a few things."

"Take your time."

She sniffed the warm, buttery aroma in the air and stepped into the living room, still clutching her dirty clothes. "Did you toast another bagel?"

He came out of the kitchen with a plate in one hand and waving a fork in the other. "I made some eggs, too. Sorry, I was starving. Do you want some?"

"No, thanks, and you don't have to apologize for eating." Her gaze tracked over his solid form. A bod like that needed more than a half a bagel to fuel it.

"I'll be done before you finish packing." His eyes widened and he pointed the fork at her. "You look...more relaxed. Are you feeling better?"

"Not much." She pressed a hand to her belly. "When I think about Dr. Fazal, I feel sick to my stomach."

"I know. I'm sorry." He dropped his gaze to the plate of steaming scrambled eggs. "I understand."

His low voice vibrated with emotion. He must've lost a few of his fellow SEALs in combat.

"But if we can do something to find his killers—" she hugged her clothes to her chest "—that will make me feel better. Justice is sweet."

"Justice is...justice." He stabbed a clump of eggs with his fork. "Start packing."

She accomplished the task in twenty minutes and when she came into the kitchen, Austin had washed and dried all the dishes.

"Wow, a navy SEAL and handy in the kitchen. Thanks."

He snapped his fingers. "Nothing to it. I grew up on a ranch with three brothers and two sisters, and we were all expected to do the chores—outside and inside."

"A ranch?" She nudged one of his cowboy

boots planted firmly on her floor. "That explains these. Where's the ranch?"

"Wyoming."

"Never been there."

"You're a city girl, huh?"

She shrugged. "Never had a chance to be anything else."

"Ready?" He took the handle of her wheeled suitcase. "My hotel first, and then I'll drop you off at the office. We'll get you there by twelve fifteen."

"Hang on." She charged across the room and swept the framed photo of her and Dr. Fazal from the TV stand and stuffed it into the side compartment of her suitcase.

As they got to the door, she turned and took in her small apartment, her first place all to herself, her refuge.

"You'll be back."

The reality of her situation hit her again when Austin crouched beneath her car to search for bugs. He popped up, brushing the seat of his jeans. "Just want to make sure they weren't busy in the night."

"And were they?"

He spread his empty hands in front of her. "Not this time."

He slid into the driver's seat since he'd be dropping her off. It felt strange giving over so much control to someone so quickly, but she almost felt like her life depended on it—and maybe it did.

As they got closer to downtown, her stomach tightened into knots. Could she return to the place where someone had shot and killed Dr. Fazal?

Her phone buzzed and she peered at the screen. "I think it's the Boston PD."

"Answer it."

"Hello?"

"Ms. Grant? This is Detective Marvin."

"Yes, hello, detective."

"We're done collecting evidence in the office, and you're free to return."

"One of the nurses already told me. We're all meeting there after noon."

"Good. Let us know if you come across anything."

"We will."

"And, Ms. Grant?"

"Yes?"

"Dr. Fazal shot himself."

"No!" Her hand curled around her phone so tightly, the edges cut into her palm. "That's ridiculous. You saw the office."

Austin had put his hand on her thigh, his eyebrows raised to his hairline.

"I said he shot himself. I didn't say he committed suicide. We'll look at all possibilities."

"Nothing you say will make me believe Dr. Fazal killed himself after upending his own office."

Austin had sucked in a breath.

The detective ended the call and Sophia reported to Austin what he'd said. "Someone could've shot him and then placed the gun near his hand, right?"

"Yes. Without seeing the evidence report, it's hard to figure out what happened." He squeezed her leg. "It's like I said before, Sophia. Dr. Fazal would've taken his own life before he'd allow himself to be questioned and probably tortured."

"Before he'd give up what they wanted? Because we know they wanted more than his death. You said that yourself."

"I still believe it." He tapped the windshield. "I'm in the next block."

He wheeled her car into the circular front drive of a large chain hotel. "I'll check with the valet to see if we can leave the car here for thirty minutes."

Austin exited the car and cleared things with the valet before waving at her. Seemed as if the attendant had a hard time saying no to Austin, too.

Austin popped her trunk and the valet lifted

her suitcase and laptop from inside. Austin pressed some money into the valet's hand and grabbed her suitcase.

They breezed past the reception desk and landed in front of the elevator. He punched the button and looked over his shoulder. "That's another good thing about having you stay here. You don't have to check in and leave a trail."

What was the other good thing? She let that question pass as she stepped into the elevator. "Leave a trail? You mean, like a credit card? I know enough not to use a credit card if someone's following me."

"Doesn't matter if you pay with cash. It's that interaction. Until we know who we're dealing with, we have to expect a high level of sophistication. They've already identified and bugged your car, located and broke into your apartment. These are no amateurs."

"And killed Dr. Fazal." She slumped against the wall of the elevator car.

"They're not going to get away with it." His jaw tightened and a glitter of anger sparked in his green eyes.

She could almost believe him, but people got away with stuff all the time. She'd had a couple of sets of foster parents who'd gotten away with plenty.

The car finally stopped on the fourteenth

floor, and the doors whisked open. She pressed the button to hold the doors open as Austin wheeled her bag out of the elevator. She followed him halfway down the hallway, and he stopped in front of a room across from the ice maker.

He fished a card out of his pocket and held it up. "Home sweet home for the time being, although I've spent all of ten minutes here."

He slid the card home and pushed open the door, holding it open for her. When she crossed the threshold, her gaze skimmed across the king-size bed. Was this the other good thing about having her stay here?

He parked her suitcase in the corner and transferred her laptop from the top of the suitcase to a desk by the window. "That sofa folds out to a bed, by the way, and I'll be bunking there."

She shouldn't have expected anything less from this chivalrous cowboy, even though she'd never met anyone quite like him.

"It's your room and you're a lot bigger than I am. You keep the bed and I'll take the sofa bed."

"We'll figure it out later." He shrugged out of his jacket. "Right now I'm going to shower and change. We have an hour before you need to be at the office."

"We'll have plenty of time. The office isn't

far from here." She stood at the window, pressing her forehead against the glass. Somewhere out there, Dr. Fazal's killers lurked, waiting for their chance to strike at her. Could she trust Austin to protect her?

Biting her bottom lip, she turned to watch him pulling clothes out of his suitcase. Right now she didn't have a choice.

He glanced up, folding his arms over a pair of jeans. "Are you okay? I won't be long. You can help yourself to the minibar, courtesy of the US government."

She rolled her eyes. "I've had enough from the government. I'm good."

He disappeared into the bathroom, and she plugged in her laptop and powered it up. She scrolled through her emails and tripped across another one from Tyler, the guy she'd stood up last night.

They'd been chatting back and forth for a few weeks and had met face-to-face over coffee. She at least owed him an explanation. She composed a quick email letting him know a friend had passed away unexpectedly and they could reschedule later if he was still interested.

She clicked Send and then buried her chin in the palm of her hand as she wedged her elbow on the desk. Was she still interested?

Everything about Austin Foley had overwhelmed her senses from the second he popped up in her back seat. Of course, Austin wasn't real. He'd appeared like a knight in shining armor just when she'd been plunged into darkness and despair—and he'd disappear just as suddenly once he learned what he was here to learn. She'd probably still be dealing with the darkness and despair once he'd vanished. Dr. Fazal was gone.

The bathroom door opened behind her, followed by a burst of citrus steam. She twisted around in her chair.

Austin peered at her from the folds of the white towel engulfing his head. "I left my shirt in here."

Lucky her. As he toweled his hair, she tried not to stare at the muscles that rippled across his bare chest and abs.

He tossed the towel onto the bed and crouched in front of his suitcase, pawing through the contents. "I'm glad I packed some long sleeves and flannels. It's still cold even though spring's right around the corner."

She took in his back and the way his broad shoulders narrowed to his waist in a perfect V. The man didn't have an ounce of fat on his body.

He twisted his head over one of those broad shoulders and heat crested over her face. She turned back to her laptop on the desk. "Yeah, cold for spring."

He whistled some tuneless melody and slammed the bathroom door several seconds later.

She covered her still-warm face with both of her hands. She needed to get a grip. Austin probably had a wife and children—he still looked young. Navy SEALs had families, didn't they? He would. He seemed like the God, country, family type all over. She'd already checked out his bare ring finger, but that didn't mean anything. He probably removed his wedding ring on assignment. Hell, he probably used his stellar hotness to gain cooperation from female witnesses like her.

She spun around when he returned to the room, his coppery brown hair damp and shiny, his face freshly shaved.

"How often do you do assignments like this?"

"Assignments like this?" He cocked his head. "What do you mean?"

"You know." She flapped her hands in the air. "Skullduggery and protecting unsuspecting witnesses and…investigating stuff."

"This is my first and most likely last time."

"Really?"

"Sophia, I'm in the US Navy. I'm supposed to be operating overseas on missions approved by the Department of Defense. I am absolutely not supposed to be conducting any type of surveillance or covert actions on home soil."

"So, why are you?"

"I was asked...ordered by higher-ranking personnel than my commanding officers. I thought I had made that clear. I report to some faceless woman—or at least I think she's a woman—named Ariel. I'm here because I'd been instrumental in spiriting Dr. Fazal out of Pakistan."

"If you got caught by the police, would these high-ranking personnel stand by you? Bail you out? Or would they hang you out to dry?"

"I'm not going to get caught by the police—or anyone else."

He'd just answered her question. He was on his own, and the same authority figures who'd ordered him stateside to protect Dr. Fazal would disown him in a second to protect their own backsides. He knew it...and didn't care.

She tapped her computer screen. "It's almost twelve o'clock. Are you ready?"

"Shoes." He swept up a pair of running shoes from the floor and sat on the edge of the bed to put them on.

"No lucky cowboy boots today?"

"Lucky?" He grinned in a kind of aw-shucks way, and an answering smile tugged at her lips.

"I don't know. We've been having pretty good luck with you wearing those boots."

"These might be lucky, too." He tied one shoe and stomped it on the carpet. "Might have to do some walking this afternoon."

"There's a coffee place about a half a block down from the office building."

"I noticed it before. That's where I'll be when you finish cleaning up the office."

It didn't take them long to get from the hotel to the medical office building, and Sophia used her parking card to get into the lot. She directed Austin to a different level from where she usually parked just in case her stalkers were looking out for her car.

When they stopped at the elevator, Austin held out his hand. "Let me have your phone. I'll put my number in your contacts, but I'll be waiting for you at the coffee place, so just come on over when you're done."

He tapped his number into her phone and held it out to her when he finished.

She glanced at the new contact. "Supreme Dry Cleaners?"

"That's me." He raised his right hand. "Just in case someone ever gets hold of your phone."

A little shiver zipped across the back of her neck. This espionage stuff was getting too real for comfort. "Got it. See you in about an hour."

He pushed through the metal door to take the steps to the street level, and she stabbed the elevator button to call the car. As she watched the door slam behind Austin, her stomach flip-flopped just like it had last night when he'd left her before the cops arrived.

In less than twenty-four hours, Austin Foley had become a crutch for her, a security blanket, a required accessory...like a cell phone or a purse. She didn't like it.

When the elevator doors opened on the floor of the office, she closed her eyes and took a deep breath before stepping out. If the other residents on the floor had been rubbernecking into Dr. Fazal's office, they must've gotten their fill already because all the doors on the hallway were firmly closed. Of course, not many of the doctors worked on Saturday.

A crumpled ribbon of crime scene tape pooled on the floor in front of the office, and she stepped over it as she entered the waiting room. She released a noisy breath as Ginny, in jeans and tennis shoes, jumped up from the floor.

"Oh, my God, Sophia. I can't believe this happened." Ginny wrapped her in a hug, rocking her back and forth. "I know how close you were to Dr. Fazal, and you had to find him. I'm so sorry. I'm so sorry for all of us."

Sophia patted Ginny's back. "I-it's terrible. Have you called all the patients?"

Ginny gave her a final squeeze before releasing her. "Don't worry about that. I called everyone who had appointments this week. I referred them all to Dr. Bishop, and I talked to him, as well. I'll take care of the rest of the patients later."

"Morgan and Anna?"

"Morgan's in the back and Anna's not in yet." She swept her arm across the waiting room. "I've been cleaning up the reception area. There wasn't much out of place in the waiting room, but then all we have are magazines and pamphlets up here. Still, they rifled through those, too. What in the world were they looking for among our magazine racks?"

"Obviously not drugs." Sophia pressed her lips together. She didn't want to give anything away about the motive for the killing, but some things were obvious.

"Maybe his killer was already drug-addled and just went crazy."

At least Ginny wasn't spouting the ridiculous suicide theory. "Have you seen the cops yet?"

"I was here when they finished gathering their evidence. You know Dr. Fazal's computer was stolen?"

"I told the police that last night."

"And all the drugs." Morgan poked her head out of the supply room. "So, maybe Ginny's theory is correct. Some junkies broke in here, grabbed the meds, maybe demanded more and when Dr. Fazal didn't give them up, they shot him."

"There was nothing to *give up*." Sophia squeezed the back of her neck. "What else could Dr. Fazal give them?"

Morgan shook her head. "I don't know. It looks like they searched through everything. I suppose you've seen your office since you were here last night. That must've been horrible."

"It was." Sophia brushed a hand across her eyes. "I'm going to see what's what in my office. If Anna doesn't show up, I'll help you with the rest when I'm done."

"I'm here." Anna stumbled into the waiting room with tears streaming down her face. "I can't believe this."

Ginny gave Anna a bear hug and the two women clung together for a few minutes, their tears mingling. Their unbridled emotion socked her in the gut. Sophia didn't even know how to break down like that, wouldn't even know how, and witnessing their pain and grief only made her shell grow harder.

She slipped away from the cryfest and stepped into her office. She maneuvered around the two chairs facing her desk and sank into the chair behind it. She powered on the computer and rested her fingers on the keyboard while she waited for it to come to life.

Why had Dr. Fazal's killers taken only his computer? They probably figured they'd be too conspicuous lugging a host of computers out of the office, although apparently nobody had seen them leave.

She went through her email and opened a few files, but she didn't know what she was looking for. Sighing, she dropped to her knees and gathered up the papers and file folders littering the floor.

They'd probably stolen the drugs to make it look like a typical crime, although they had to know the FBI would be keeping tabs on Dr. Fazal, or at least would be alerted in the event of his murder.

What did they want? What secrets had Hamid been keeping? What secrets had he been keeping from her?

She plopped back in the chair and spun it around to face her bookshelf. The books had been rifled through, too. So, had they been searching for something on paper? A computer file? From the looks of the office, they didn't know.

She ran her hands down the spines of the

books to straighten them on the shelf. Then she leaned forward to retrieve a couple that had been left on the floor.

A bright pink sticky note beneath the desk caught her eye. She slid from the chair to the floor and reached for it. Still beneath the desk, she peered at the note, wrinkling her nose as she recognized Dr. Fazal's scratchy handwriting. She clambered back into the chair and held the note under the desk lamp.

As she deciphered the words, her heart slammed against her rib cage. Dr. Fazal had left her a clue.

Chapter Six

Austin flexed his fingers before attacking the keyboard. Entering *Peter Patel* in the search engine returned multiple pages and too many entries to count.

He tried narrowing it down by entering the data from the patient file but didn't get any hits.

Slumping in his chair, he stretched his legs out to the side and took a careful sip of coffee. It beat the stuff Sophia had brewed in that old coffeemaker of hers, but that concoction suited her—strong, bracing and no frills.

Would she keep up that strong front back at the office where she'd discovered Dr. Fazal's body? None of this could be easy for her, and yet she'd responded like a soldier.

How far would Fazal's killers go to contact Sophia, and what exactly did they want from her?

Someone like Sophia wouldn't go for any

type of witness protection, but how could they keep her safe in Boston if these guys were determined to interrogate her...or worse? How could *he* keep her safe?

The key could be this guy, Patel. He sat up and grabbed his phone, and then hunched over the laptop to scroll to Patel's phone number from the file.

He tapped the number into his cell and listened to the phone on the other end of the line ring and ring. Patel didn't even have voice mail? If this were a cell phone number, a recording would come on indicating the person hadn't set up voice mail.

He jotted down Patel's address on a napkin, and then entered it into the computer. The location in Brookline wasn't too far. If Patel wouldn't answer his phone, Austin would pay him a surprise visit.

He accessed his email and pored over the new pictures of his nephew his sister had sent. This baby made him an uncle six times, and he had fun with the role even though he knew his turn would have to wait. His family didn't even know he was stateside, and he couldn't tell them. There was a lot he couldn't tell his family.

The door to the coffeehouse flew open and he glanced up, his heart doing a flip-flop when he saw Sophia's pale face framed by her disheveled black hair.

He kicked out the chair across from him and she dropped into it, waving a pink square of paper in his face. "I found something."

"What is it?"

She smacked the sticky note on the table next to his laptop. "It *is* Patel, and Dr. Fazal was trying to warn me."

He peeled the note from the table and held it close to his face, his eyebrows colliding over his nose. "What the hell does this say?"

"Shh." She put her finger to her lips and looked to her right and then to her left. She leaned forward pointing at each word upside down as she read it out to him in a whisper.

"Leave. New. Patient. Files."

"Is that what that says?" He flicked the edge of the note. "I'm underwhelmed. What does it mean and how is it a warning?"

She ripped the note from the table and pressed it to her heart. "He's telling me to leave the new patient files alone, and the new patient is?"

"Peter Patel."

"That's right. He's the only new patient who hasn't been entered in the database, so it would only apply to him. Also, this is not something I'd normally handle. It's Ginny's responsibility to enter patient files into the database."

"Where did you find this note? You hadn't seen it before...before his murder?"

"No. It wasn't there when I left my office that night. I found it beneath my desk, where it must've floated when my office was trashed."

"Is this—" his eyes dropped to the note still pressed against her breast "—a typical way for him to communicate with you? Sticky notes?"

"Not unheard of, but not something he'd do frequently. It would definitely get my attention, and don't you see? It's cryptic enough that nobody else would consider it important or out of the ordinary."

"Cryptic for you as well, but gets the job done. The only reason I can think of that he'd warn you off Patel is if he believed Patel would reach out to you."

She covered her mouth with the pink square. "Do you think that was Patel last night in Cambridge with the gun?"

"I don't know." He swirled the coffee in his cup. "If Patel came to see Dr. Fazal, maybe to warn him about something, and Fazal was protecting him by pretending he was a patient, I just can't see someone like that harming you. Dr. Fazal would never do that to you."

"But Patel might try to reach out to me, anyway?"

"If Dr. Fazal knew he was a dead man, he

might want to warn you away from Patel just to keep you out of the loop. Patel could be a desperate man. Once he hears about Fazal's murder, he might turn to you instead. Maybe Fazal is warning you against that inevitability."

"He was thinking of me even at the end." She cupped the note between her two hands, almost as if in prayer.

"He was warning *you* away from Patel." He tapped the napkin with Patel's address. "Not me."

"Are you going to track him down?"

"Yes."

"I'm coming with you."

"That's exactly what Dr. Fazal didn't want."

"Well, he misjudged his enemies if he thought they'd leave me alone. I'm in this, whether or not that's what Dr. Fazal wanted."

"Not what he wanted."

"Do you think I'll be safer in that hotel room on my own or safer with you?"

He opened his mouth and then snapped it shut. Of course she'd be safer with him. He leveled a finger at her. "If you come along with me, you need to do exactly what I say. I know you think you're street smart and savvy, but this is a different world."

"You're lucky I am street smart and savvy

because I recognized you as one of the good guys right away." She pushed his finger out of the way. "When do we go?"

"Let me wrap up a few things first. Were the police at the office when you were there cleaning up?"

"No, but Ginny, the receptionist, saw them when she got there. I gather they didn't have any news."

"What about the...uh, arrangements for Dr. Fazal?"

"The funeral?" She dropped the pink note in her purse. "Morgan told me some of his colleagues are organizing a memorial service, and they actually want me to say something. According to his religion, he needs to be buried as soon as the coroner releases his body— whenever that is. The memorial service can take place sooner."

He jerked his thumb at the counter. "Go get yourself a coffee while I finish."

"I prefer the stuff at the donut shop across the street."

His lips quirked as he suppressed a smile. "What?"

"Nothing. If you want to run across the street, I'll probably be done by the time you get back."

"I'll wait here." With one finger, she dragged

the napkin with Patel's address to her side of the table. "Brookline, huh?"

"Looks about five miles away on the directions."

"It's close." She held up her cell phone. "Do you want me to put it in my GPS?"

"Go ahead. Do you want to drive or navigate?"

"Since it's my car, I'll drive."

"I'll wear my seat belt."

She nudged his shoe with her foot. "Are you implying that I'm a lousy driver?"

"Not at all. I'm just all about safety."

The nudge turned into a kick. "Liar."

"There." He clicked Send on his request. "I just submitted Peter Patel's name to our database to see if we have anything on him."

"You don't think Peter Patel's a fake name?"

"I do, but it's worth a try. Maybe it's a fake name he's used before, so it might come up as an alias for the real person."

She tilted her head. "Is this what you do as a navy SEAL? Intelligence? Espionage?"

"Me?" He raised his eyebrows. "No, although I've had some training."

"Then, what do you do?"

"I'm a sniper."

Her dark eyes glittered as she narrowed them to slits. "You kill people from a safe distance?"

He pressed his lips into a thin line, and a muscle ticked in his jaw. "I save and protect people."

"I-is that how you protected Dr. Fazal?"

He nodded once and snapped his laptop closed. "You ready?"

"Just need to enter the address in my phone's GPS."

While she tapped her phone, he put away his laptop and tossed his cup. He didn't need to explain what he did to civilians like Sophia. He didn't imagine that she'd understand, and she shouldn't have to.

"All done." She squinted at her phone. "We should be there in seventeen minutes."

"With you driving, we could cut that down to ten."

"I'll be careful, but your concern seems pretty funny coming from a guy who takes bigger risks than traveling in a fast-moving car."

As he opened the door for her, he shook his finger. "A lot of soldiers come back from their tours and die in car accidents."

"You're right."

They walked back to the medical building parking structure and jogged up one flight of stairs to their level.

Austin pressed the car keys into her hand. "Here you go."

Clutching the key ring, she stepped back from the car. "Sh-should you check it out again?"

He pulled the bug detector from his jacket pocket and held it up. "I have something better, so I don't have to crawl beneath the car."

Pressing the button on the device, he waved it across the car's bumper, along the sides and over the hood. "All clear."

She clicked the key fob. "Wow, that's really some James Bond stuff right there."

"Naw." He stuffed the detector in his pocket. "Pretty basic, actually."

He dropped into the passenger seat beside her, and she handed him her cell phone. "Navigate, please."

As she pulled out of the parking lot, he glanced at the phone and directed her to turn right at the next lights.

On the drive to Brookline, she stayed just under the speed limit and her tires didn't squeal once.

"The address is another two blocks up on the right."

She slowed the car. "Nice neighborhood."

"It's coming up." He dropped his gaze to the phone. "Just about…"

"Are you kidding me? It's seven twenty-eight, isn't it?"

He jerked his head up and swore as they

rolled past a house under construction. "Pull over. I suppose we should've expected this. A phone number with no voice mail and an address with no house."

She parked the car and Austin jumped out. Stuffing his hands into his pockets, he approached the half-finished house.

Sophia hovered at his elbow. "Doesn't look like anyone's living here, either."

A truck rumbled up behind them, and Austin stepped to the side to allow it to pull into the dirt driveway. A man exited the truck and clapped a hardhat on his head. "Can I help you folks?"

Austin cleared his throat. "New construction or a remodel?"

"New construction. A developer bought the property and razed it. You interested? We had a buyer, but he pulled out."

Sophia asked, "Was the buyer named Patel?"

"No, ma'am. Why? Someone you know?"

"A friend. He's looking, too."

The man fished a card from his front pocket. "If you're interested, here's the number for the sales office. The developer has a few other properties in Brookline."

"Thanks." Sophia took the card and Austin nodded at the man, who turned toward the bed of his truck.

When they got back into Sophia's car, they turned to each other at the same time.

Austin smacked his knee. "Fake name, fake address, fake phone number. How are we going to find this guy?"

"Dr. Fazal's memorial service. If he was a friend, he just might show up."

"If he wants to keep a low profile, he won't show up. He might be worried the same guys who took out Fazal are now gunning for him."

"What was between those two?" She gripped the steering wheel with both hands. "Patel shows up, Dr. Fazal starts acting nervous, pretends Patel's a patient, probably to talk to him in private and cover his tracks, and then Dr. Fazal winds up dead—murdered. Why did he have to come here and stir up trouble for Hamid?"

A sob caught in her throat, and her fingers curled around the steering wheel in a death grip.

Austin brushed his knuckles down her arm and covered one of her hands with his. "Hamid was never out of trouble, Sophia. Nobody had to stir it up for him. He must've been living life with one eye on the rearview mirror ever since we got him out of Pakistan."

"But he *was* happy. He wasn't afraid—until this Patel showed up."

He squeezed her hand. "You made him happy.

He cared about you, and that gave him a reason to live and hope."

"I hope so."

"Do you need to go back to the office?"

"No. Ginny's doing the bulk of the work, notifying patients, getting their files together for the next doctor. They still need their treatment." She started the car and glanced over her left shoulder.

He placed his hand on the steering wheel. "Are you sure you don't want me to drive?"

"Why? Did I scare you on the way over?"

"Your driving was okay. My heart rate went up only once." And he didn't want to tell her that was when she'd puckered her lips to drink from her bottle of water. "You look tired and stressed."

"I am tired and stressed, but I think you just like being in control."

He shrugged and then rolled his shoulders. "I'm not gonna deny that."

"I'm good." She pulled away from the curb to prove it. "Back to the hotel?"

"Unless you have somewhere else to be?"

"I have nothing and no one right now—not even a job to go to."

"You have patients, too, right?"

"My patients are all Dr. Fazal's patients. They're not going to follow me anywhere. I'm still in training. I'll definitely have to look for another job, and with my background?" She gave a dry laugh that seemed to lodge in her throat. "That ain't gonna be easy."

He turned his head to watch the passing scenery—clumps of old snow on the side of the road and stark trees trying to form hard buds in the still crisp air. "All that stuff… It's in your past. You were practically a juvenile."

"Ah, practically, but not quite." She twisted her head around, her gaze doing a quick search of his face. "How much do you know about me?"

She focused her attention back on the road, and he studied her profile, her wide, generous mouth at odds with the hard glitter she let creep into her eyes all too often. What he knew about this woman only scratched the surface.

"Of course, we did a background check of the people closest to Dr. Fazal."

"That wouldn't be many, since he liked to keep to himself."

"I know that."

Sophia's phone buzzed between them on the console.

"Are you going to get that?"

"I may be a bad driver but I don't answer the phone when I'm behind the wheel."

His hand hovered over the phone. "Should I?"

"If it's important enough, the caller will leave a message."

Was she expecting a call from someone on that dating website? His youngest sister, who lived in LA met guys online, too. When he and his brothers had found out they'd hit the roof, but she just laughed at them. Said everyone met people like that, and it was perfectly safe. Nothing was perfectly safe. He glanced at Sophia. Especially when extremely lethal terrorists had you in their crosshairs.

When they edged into the semicircular drive in front of the hotel, he said, "It's going to be tough having two cars. Just leave it with the valet, and he'll park it."

"Valet? Are you kidding? That costs a fortune."

He rolled his eyes. "You have a thing about paying for parking, don't you?"

"It's expensive to park in Boston and spaces are at a premium."

"I'll pay for it—work-related expense."

"How long are you going to be on this job, anyway?"

"Should be hearing something about that soon."

She pulled in front of the hotel and jammed on the brakes. He jerked forward and back, his head hitting the headrest. "Wow."

"Is there a possibility that you'll be ordered to return to regular duty?"

"I was sent out here on a mission to protect Dr. Fazal—that failed."

"Okay, but…" She huffed out a breath. "Yeah, you're not supposed to be here, anyway."

She opened the car door for the valet standing at her window and snatched the ticket from him.

Austin didn't want to leave any more than Sophia wanted him to, but his job description didn't include protecting anyone but Fazal—mission over.

Sophia charged ahead, and he took long strides to follow her. Her stiff back and squared shoulders screamed anger, but he already knew her anger masked fear or disappointment. Maybe he did know Sophia better than he thought he did.

He caught up with her. "Is this a race?"

"I just want to be alone, but I can't even go back to my own apartment, can I?" She punched the elevator button with the side of her fist.

He ran his hands down her arms and she practically vibrated beneath his touch. "We'll have you back home soon."

"Yeah, when you decide to ditch this place. Then I guess I'll be free to do what I want—including die."

The elevator doors opened and he bit down

on his reply as a stream of people exited the car. Three other people entered the elevator after them, and Austin shifted toward the panel of buttons to make room.

He lowered his voice. "Did you check your call?"

"It's from Ginny, probably with some questions about the office. She left a voice mail. I'll listen to it when we get to the room."

When the elevator settled on his floor, they squeezed out of the car and walked silently to the room.

He opened the door for Sophia, and she took her phone out of her jacket pocket and wedged her shoulder against the window. She tapped her cell and listened, her eyes getting wider and wider with each second.

His pulse ratcheted up several notches. "What's wrong? What's she saying?"

"I'll let you listen." She tapped her phone and a woman's high-pitched, strained voice came over the line in a rush of words.

"Where'd you take off to so fast, Sophia? You left, Morgan left and Anna took off right after her. I was stuck doing the patient calls. Do you know how hard it was to repeat over and over that Dr. Fazal was dead?" A sob broke into her words and then she continued.

"Of course you do. You found him. And if

that wasn't stressful enough, a man came by the office and he was looking for you. I mean, really looking for you. He said he was a friend of Dr. Fazal's and he did have a similar accent. He just wouldn't take no for an answer. Finally I told him to give me his number and I'd give it to you. So here it is, but you'd better call me back before you contact him."

She recited a phone number and ended the message with an urgent "Call me."

Sophia crossed her arms. "What do you think? Is that Patel or…maybe the guy from last night?"

"I'm not sure, but you're not calling him back on your phone. You don't want him to have your number." He dragged his own phone from his pocket. "We can use mine. It can't be traced, but you'd better call Ginny first and get all the details. Is she usually…excitable?"

"She can be, but I've never heard her like that before. It could just be the added stress of contacting the patients this morning. I'll call her now."

"Speaker, please."

Sophia placed the call. It rang four times, and then a man answered.

"Hello?"

"Hello?" Sophia's eyes jumped to Austin's face. "Who's this?"

"This is Officer Kelso with the Boston PD. Are you calling Ginny Faraday?"

Austin's heart thudded in his chest, and he held his breath.

Sophia lowered herself to the edge of the chair. "Yes. Why are you answering her phone? Where's Ginny?"

"I'm sorry, ma'am. Ms. Faraday was just involved in an accident, a hit-and-run."

Sophia gasped, and Austin took two steps and crouched beside her.

"I-is she okay?"

"I'm sorry, ma'am. Ms. Faraday was fatally injured."

Chapter Seven

The man on the other end of the line kept asking questions, but Sophia had slipped into a fog. Ginny had just called her. How had this happened?

Austin took the phone from her slack fingers. "Officer Kelso, my friend is in shock. Can you tell us what happened?"

"From witness accounts, Ms. Faraday stepped off the curb and a car careened around the corner and hit her. The car took off."

Sophia hugged herself and rocked forward. An accident. It was just an accident.

"Is your friend related to Ms. Faraday?"

"No, a coworker."

"Does she know a relative we can contact? This just happened. Ms. Faraday is—is still at the scene."

Sophia closed her eyes and covered her mouth

with both hands. Death and loss. When did it ever end?

Austin poked her arm. "Next of kin for Ginny?"

Her eyes flew open. "Kara Germanski. She's Ginny's sister. I'm sure her number's in Ginny's phone."

Austin relayed the information to the cop and then ended the call. He placed her phone on the table and remained on the floor by her side.

Twisting her head toward him, she whispered, "Unbelievable. How can someone just run over a human being and leave her in the street?"

"Sophia."

"No." She covered her ears.

"Ginny was murdered."

She doubled over and touched her forehead to her knees. "Why? Why would he hurt her? She took his number, gave it to me."

"We don't know that the man she spoke to was the one driving the car or even if they were working together. Maybe the number you have is Peter Patel's. Maybe someone saw her talking to Patel and took care of business."

He put a hand on her bouncing knee. "We need to go back to the office and retrace her steps. I need to get hold of that accident report to see if there were any witnesses who said any- thing about the car or the driver."

She poked at the phone with her fingertip, scooting it away from her. "Should I call him now?"

"No. Let's go to the office first. Are you going to tell the nurses?"

"Oh, my God. I can't handle that right now. Anna is going to fall apart." She ran her hands across her face to make sure *she* wasn't falling apart. "Do you think the police are going to connect Ginny's death to Dr. Fazal's?"

"Any good detective would. They'll inves- tigate it."

"Should we go back now?"

"I need to make a few phone calls first. Do you want something from the minibar or the vending machines?"

"Is that a hint to get me out of the room?"

"Or I can leave."

She pushed up from the chair and swept past him. "I'll get a soda from the machine. Do you want something?"

"Anything with caffeine. Do you need some money?"

"I got it." When she stepped into the hall- way and the door slammed behind her, she leaned against the wall. She couldn't believe this was happening.

She thought she'd left the violence and ugliness behind her when she'd finally gotten away from the south side. Hadn't everyone always told her if she finished school, got a degree and found a good job trouble would stop following her? She'd done all of that, and it looked like trouble had found her, anyway. It always would.

She launched herself off the wall and crossed the hall to the room with the ice and vending machines.

She braced her hands against the buzzing machine, hanging her head between her arms. If Austin was in there getting orders to abandon this mission and return overseas where he belonged, she'd be in real trouble.

Did the US government care about that? Care about her? She puffed out a breath. Who was she kidding? When had any government entity ever cared about what happened to her? Child Protective Services had failed her at every turn.

Austin cared. She hadn't been imagining that, but he'd disappear in a flash if his superiors ordered him to scrap the mission.

She fed a dollar bill into the machine and selected a diet soda for herself. Then she put another bill in and punched the button for a soda for Austin. She couldn't blame him if he had to follow orders.

Maybe she could ask the sniper for some

shooting pointers before he left. She needed the practice.

When she returned to the room, she held out a can to Austin, stretched out on the bed, his arms crossed behind his head. "Caffeinated, as you requested."

He curled his hand around the can, his fingers pressing against hers so that they were both holding on to the can. His eyes met hers across the space between them. "Good news."

"They caught Dr. Fazal's killers, Ginny's killers and I'm completely out of danger."

His lips twisted. "Why'd you do that? Now my news isn't going to make an impression."

"Try me." She pulled her hand away from his and popped the tab on her own can.

"After I told my commanding officer everything that was going down out here, he checked with Ariel, who authorized me to stay at least until I can identify Peter Patel."

"That is good news." Taking a sip from her can, she turned away from him so that he couldn't see just how much that news meant to her. She had to play it cool because soon he would leave—even if it wasn't today.

"I'm ready, even though it doesn't look like it." Austin swung his legs off the side of the bed. "Do you want to walk over or drive?"

"Might as well walk. I could use the fresh air to clear my head."

"Me, too." He held up his can. "We can drink and walk at the same time."

She slipped her jacket from the back of the chair. "Do you think the cops will still be at the scene? Ginny won't still be there, will she?"

He glanced at the alarm clock by the side of the bed. "It's a fatality. An accident-investigation team will be at the scene for hours…and Ginny's body will be, too. Do you want to give it another few hours?"

"It'll be getting dark in a few hours." She stuffed her arms into the sleeves of her jacket. "Besides, you want to talk to the cops, right?"

"They're not going to talk to me until I get some sort of approval from the FBI. Since the FBI doesn't want to acknowledge I'm here looking into Fazal, that's not going to happen, but I can look at the accident scene myself."

With their sodas in hand, they stepped outside the hotel and into a cool, sharp breeze. Sophia flipped up the collar of her jacket while glancing over her shoulder.

"Are you okay?"

"I'm just wondering who's watching and following." She hunched her shoulders. "Someone must've been watching Ginny. The man who approached her, whether that's Patel or not, must've known the other two had left."

"Oh, they're out there." He gulped down the rest of his drink and crushed the can in one hand. "I'm just wondering if they know you have a bodyguard."

"Is that what you are?" She lifted one eyebrow, liking the sound of his job description.

"The man who approached you in Cambridge might just think I got lucky in disarming him."

"Lucky? Yeah, I can't see your average accountant or engineer taking down a guy with a gun like that."

"Of course, they might be wondering why we took off when the officer arrived on the scene and why you never reported the incident."

"The first they do know, but how would they know whether or not I reported the incident? We could've taken off because we didn't realize the man approaching us was a cop."

"True, but don't be so sure they don't know what's going on with the Boston PD."

She choked on her soda and it fizzed in her nose. "Really? They would have access to that information?"

"Online information is out there for the taking—as long as you know how to access it."

"That's a scary thought."

"Don't you periodically get emails from stores

or government agencies telling you that your personal information has been compromised? It's the same thing—hackers hacking."

"Nothing's safe, is it?"

He tugged on her purse strap. "You're safe—with me."

She stretched her lips into a smile. The way she'd felt when she discovered that Austin might be leaving proved that she wasn't safe with him at all. How had she grown so dependent on him when she hadn't even known him two days ago? She'd never been this dependent on anyone before—except Dr. Fazal.

They spotted the accident scene a block away. Emergency vehicles formed a barrier around the corner. Sophia swallowed when she saw the coroner's van.

Her steps dragged, and Austin touched her shoulder. "Do you want to wait in the coffee-house, or better yet, the donut shop?"

"No."

Austin's hand dropped to the small of her back and he kept it there as they drew closer to the scene, and she had no intention of shrugging it off.

They hung out on the fringes of the crowd still clustered around the corner. Sophia couldn't see Ginny's body and didn't want to.

Austin turned to the man next to him. "What happened?"

"Hit-and-run. Car hit a pedestrian, and he died."

The guy in front of the stranger cranked his head over his shoulder. "She. It was a woman."

Austin whistled. "Anyone see it happen? Anyone get a look at the car?"

The shorter man in front answered again. "Not that I heard."

Austin took her arm and put his lips close to her ear. "Let's retrace her steps."

Leading the way, Austin led her through a clutch of people that had formed behind them, and they walked through the front door of the office building.

"Did Ginny drive?"

"She took the T in." She jerked her thumb over her shoulder. "I'm sure she was on her way to the T stop one block up."

They took the elevator up to the office, and she unlocked the door. Ginny and the others had done a good job of cleaning up.

She stood in the middle of the waiting room and turned around. "This room wasn't that messed up—nothing to search, but I noticed the magazines had been rifled."

"So, they could've been looking for something flat, a piece of paper or a disk of some sort." Austin thumbed through a celebrity magazine and then stuffed it back in the rack.

She pulled open the door to the back office and gestured to her right. "This was Ginny's domain, the reception area. They trashed this."

"She didn't say on the phone where the man approached her looking for you, did she? In the office or outside?"

"No, but I'm pretty sure she would've kept the office door locked once the other two left. She'd been making patient calls."

"So, he knocked or waylaid her when she left the office." He tipped his head toward the back of the room. "Do you want to show me your office and how Dr. Fazal's body was positioned?"

She squeezed past him and stepped into her office. "This is my space. I found the pink sticky note under my desk, here."

He got on his hands and knees and peered beneath her desk. "If it became unstuck when the intruders started searching in here, it probably floated to the floor and they never saw it."

"Even if they did see it?" She shook her head. "It wouldn't have meant anything to them. That's why Dr. Fazal wrote it that way. He didn't want me talking to Patel…and I'm going to do just that."

"Dr. Fazal had no way of knowing I'd be here to help you."

"I think he would've approved. I know he held the guys who rescued him in high regard. I just never knew it was the SEALs."

"*He* was the hero. He sacrificed everything—his home, his safety—to help us bring down a very dangerous man."

She blinked. "Do you want to see where I found him?"

"Yes."

She led him to the doctor's office, which Ginny and Anna had put back together. Sophia laced her fingers in front of her, twisting them into knots as she moved around the desk. They'd never get rid of that blood on the carpet.

"There. He was lying on his back, the gun next to his hand."

Austin crouched down and looked beneath the desk. "Did it look like he was down before the room was tossed? I mean, did you notice papers on top of him or beneath him? The cops would note that, but probably didn't tell you."

"I think the search went on after his death. I just had that impression. The picture was beneath his leg, but that was the only thing I noticed. It was as if he grabbed it or swept it from the desk when he fell."

"That framed picture of the two of you? The one with the broken glass?"

"Yes, the officer allowed me to take it with me that night."

Tapping his chin, Austin rose to his feet and took a turn around the room. "You said he kept a gun in his drawer?"

"Yes, but I don't know if it was the one in his hand. Maybe he went for it and had just enough time to shoot himself. I know he wouldn't have killed himself without a good reason—a noble reason."

"He ruined their plans. They expected to get information from him and he made sure they'd never get it."

"But they obviously didn't find it if they came after me and then… Ginny."

"They killed Ginny. I don't think the man in Cambridge went after you with the same intention." He pointed at her. "They think you know something or that Dr. Fazal gave you something."

"I don't and he didn't." She wrung her hands. "Can't I just tell them…?"

"No! That won't work. Do you think they'll believe you? They might believe you after a few hours or a few days of…" He ran a hand through his short hair.

She didn't want him to finish that sentence. She didn't want to imagine what they'd do to her if they captured her. The thought of it had been enough to make Dr. Fazal put a gun to his head and pull the trigger.

She rubbed the scar on the inside of her left forearm. She wouldn't be able to endure it.

Austin looked around the room and peppered her with more questions, but none of the questions or her answers brought them any closer to figuring out what Dr. Fazal had been hiding from his killers—if anything.

"Okay, let's follow Ginny's probable path down to the street and see if we can discover anything."

"Do you think she's still down there? It's getting dark." Sophia pressed her palm against the windowpane. The office faced a different direction from the front entrance.

"Most likely. It can take hours for an accident investigation to wrap up in the case of a fatality." She watched his reflection in the window as he approached her from behind.

He looked almost unreal, like an apparition she'd conjured from her imagination. Then he touched her shoulder blade and she knew he was real…and he was the only thing standing between her and utter devastation and collapse.

"Are you ready?"

Her eyes met his in the glass and she nodded.

They exited the office, and as she locked the door behind her, the elevator opened on the floor. A vacuum cleaner poked its nose out of the door followed by Norm.

"Hey, Norm. Did you hear about what happened to Ginny?"

"I did hear, Sophia." He shook his head. "Crazy Boston drivers, and he didn't even stop."

Austin pressed the elevator button with his knuckle to hold it open. "You didn't happen to see anything, did you?"

"No. I haven't left the building since I came on duty a few hours ago. I just heard the sirens and a few people in the office were talking about it. Damn shame." He shook his head. "She must've been still upset about her argument up here. She probably wasn't paying any attention."

Sophia's heart jumped. "Argument? On this floor?"

"She was talking to a man in the hallway." Norm rolled the vacuum a few feet forward. "Right here."

"What did he look like?" Austin had let the elevator go and was focused on Norm like a laser.

Norm ducked his head. "Dark skin, dark hair, medium height. He had an accent, kind of like Dr. Fazal's. I figured it was a friend of Dr. Fazal's."

"Had you ever seen him here before?"

Norm licked his lips and glanced at Sophia.

"This is Detective French, Norm. He was looking into the accident."

"Oh, okay. I never seen him here before, but he sounded like the doctor. I thought maybe he was upset about, you know...the murder."

Sophia put her hand on Austin's arm. His intensity was going to send Norm running for the stairwell. She asked, "Did you overhear any part of the argument?"

"Naw, they were quiet. Just sort of whispering back and forth, but I could tell they were having a disagreement about something."

"You don't think this man could've been the one driving the car that hit Ginny, do you?"

Norm's eyebrows jumped. "I thought that was an accident. Someone hit Ginny on purpose?"

"We don't know that for sure." Austin crossed his arms. "So, how about it? Could the man talking to Ginny have had enough time to go down to the street, get in a car and drive around to the front before Ginny got to the corner?"

"No. No way." He leaned on the vacuum cleaner handle. "He got in the elevator with her. They went down together. So, unless she took some big detour when she got to the sidewalk, he probably left her right before she crossed the street and got hit. He could've even witnessed it."

"Okay, Norm. Thanks."

"Thank you. I appreciate it." Austin shook Norm's hand.

"Do you have a card or something? The detective who was here for Dr. Fazal gave me his card in case I remembered anything else."

Austin made a show of patting his front pocket. "Fresh out. Ms. Grant knows how to reach me."

Norm turned and trundled down the hallway, pushing his vacuum cleaner in front of him and muttering. "I sure hope the hit-and-run was just an accident. 'Cause if it wasn't, there's something hinky going on with this building and that office."

Austin called the elevator again, and when they stepped inside, they looked at each other.

Wedging his shoulder against the mirrored wall, Austin said, "The man arguing with Ginny was Patel, but is he working with someone else who ran down Ginny? Of course, why run her down if she'd given Patel your info? Patel would've had to signal someone that he'd come up short. It all happened too fast."

"In which case, the guy in the car who hit Ginny is not working with Patel." She held out her phone, tilting it back and forth. "And now I have Patel's number."

"Are you ready to call him?"

"What should I say?"

"Tell him who you are, and ask him what he wants. Don't let on that you already know about him. Play dumb."

"That's not going to be very hard to do since I have no idea what he wants." The elevator opened onto the lobby floor and she stepped out first, still clutching her phone. "Now?"

"Let's get back to the hotel so we can have some privacy. I'm going to be listening to every word on Speaker, and my phone has the ability to record the conversation, too."

Sophia pushed through the lobby door first and stepped onto the sidewalk, glancing to her left. The emergency vehicles were still there, although not as many, and the crowd had thinned. As dusk had settled, the accident investigators had lit up the area with bright white lights, giving the scene the quality of a movie set. She wished it were just a movie, not her reality… not Ginny's.

Hunching her shoulders, she huddled into her jacket. As they drew up beside the accident scene, Sophia noticed the coroner's van, no longer blocked by the fire engine, and beside it a gurney draped with a white sheet.

A gust of wind whipped down the street and lifted a corner of the sheet at the top of the gurney. For a moment, Ginny's red hair streamed freely in the breeze.

Sophia gulped back a scream and stumbled heavily against Austin's body.

He caught her around the waist and pulled her close, steadying her against his solid frame. "It's okay. You're going to be okay."

Was she? Or had her violent past caught up with her and wrapped its icy fingers around her throat again?

Chapter Eight

Through some miracle he made it back to the hotel without having to sweep up Sophia in his arms and carry her for five blocks—not that he would've minded.

She must've gotten a glimpse of Ginny on the stretcher. He should've taken her out of the building a different way. She hadn't said one word to him during their walk back. She'd allowed him to keep hold of her and guide her as they walked.

He had to get her out of Boston, away from this investigation. If the men who'd killed Fazal thought she had something they wanted, they'd never let her escape.

When they got to the room, Sophia collapsed into the chair by the window.

"Do you want something? Water? I think there are some tea bags by the coffeemaker."

Without answering, she closed her eyes.

When a few minutes passed, he thought she'd fallen asleep. Then she wriggled upright in the chair, and her eyelids flew open.

"I have to call Patel now."

"Patel can wait. You need food."

"I'm not hungry." She brushed her hair back from her face and gathered it in a ponytail in one hand. "I need to contact Patel and ask him what the hell he's doing here and why he brought this misery down on Dr. Fazal. I need to ask him what he said to upset Ginny and if he got her killed. I need to demand answers, and I'm gonna get them."

"Hang on." He held up one hand as he marveled at her quick turnaround. What resources had she just mustered to come out of her shock and fear over Ginny's death? "You don't have to do anything right now until you feel better."

"Oh, I'm fine." Her glittering dark eyes kindled with sparks of anger. "Dr. Fazal and Ginny are dead. There's nothing I can do for them now except get justice—and that justice starts with Patel."

He scratched his chin. He knew exactly how she felt. Hell, he'd lived it after his brother died.

"Are you ready to do this? Ready to keep your temper?" He squared his shoulders and looked deep into her fathomless eyes. "Because if you're not, you can blow the whole thing sky-high. You want answers from Patel, you're going to have to come in with a measured approach. Can you do that?"

She took a deep breath and released it slowly, rolling her shoulders. "I can do it."

He removed his phone from the charger and handed it to her. "Then do it."

"Do I have to do anything special to record the conversation?" She eyed the phone cupped in her hand.

"It's all set up to record and it's already on Speaker. All you have to do is enter the number Ginny gave you."

She swept her thumb across her phone's display and then tapped a number into his phone. The phone rang three times.

"Hello?" a man answered in accented English.

"Hello? Is this Mr. Patel?"

"Who is this?"

"This is Sophia Grant. My coworker Ginny Faraday gave me your number."

"Is she dead?"

Sophia's eyes flew to Austin's face, and he nodded.

"Sh-she is. It was a hit-and-run accident. How did you know that?"

"It happened right after I spoke to her." He cleared his throat. "Do you know who I am?"

She raised her brows at him and he mouthed *Dr. Fazal* and *patient*.

"I do recognize your name from Dr. Fazal's patient files. Y-you know what happened to him, don't you?"

Patel let out a sigh. "That's why I'm calling you, Ms. Grant. May I call you Sophia? I feel like I know you from Hamid's letters."

"His letters? I thought you were his patient."

"Sophia, your life is in danger."

"Because of Dr. Fazal's murder? Was Ginny's death an accident?"

"No. I'm sorry. It's all my fault. I should've never come here."

"Are you going to tell me why Dr. Fazal and Ginny were murdered? Why I'm in danger?"

"Not over the telephone. Are you on a cell phone?"

"Yes, but…" She put a hand over her mouth. "But I have complete privacy."

He choked out something between a laugh and a sob. "There is no privacy with these people."

"What people? Who are they?"

"Meet me tonight."

"Tonight?"

Austin nodded. He'd be with her every step of the way.

"Ten o'clock. I'll be wearing a baseball cap

you Americans like so much, a Boston Red Sox cap and a red scarf."

Austin glanced at the clock. They had four hours to kill.

"Ten o'clock. Where?"

"Hamid's favorite place in Boston…and come alone."

Patel ended the call, leaving her with her mouth hanging open.

"Cryptic but not very practical." He scratched the stubble on his chin, as his stomach growled.

Sophia placed his phone on the table and traced its edges with the tip of her finger. "I know exactly where he means."

"Dr. Fazal's favorite place in Boston? A restaurant? A park?" God, he hoped it was a restaurant.

"The Old North Church." She scooted forward in her seat, her eyes shining. "That was also Patel's way of assuring me he was Dr. Fazal's friend. A friend would know that about him."

"Wouldn't the church be closed at ten o'clock at night?"

"I don't imagine he means inside the church."

"Which is a shame because it would be a lot easier to keep watch in an enclosed area."

"He told me to come alone." She sucked in

her bottom lip, her eyebrows forming a V over her nose.

He swept his phone from the table and saved the recording of the conversation. "You can't think I'm going to let you go meet him by yourself."

"If he sees you, he might take off."

"He's not gonna see me." He pocketed his phone. "Is there someplace outside the church where you think he's going to be, or are you supposed to wander aimlessly around the perimeter looking for a Red Sox fan?"

"Across from the church's main entrance there's a small square. There are also a few benches beneath some trees before you get to the square. He could be there. Unless there's an event at the church tonight, there won't be many tourists mingling around."

"We're going to check it out before the meeting—on our way to get something to eat. I'm starving. I can sort out a plan to watch you to make sure nobody tries to disrupt your conversation with Patel. You might try to ask him his real name while you're at it."

"Should I tell him about you?"

"See how the conversation goes. If he has information, we need to know about it. He might be relieved to turn it over to us, and we can offer protection."

"Your protection didn't help Dr. Fazal."

His jaw tightened as he turned away from her. He didn't need any reminders of his failure. He could manage that on his own.

SOPHIA JUMPED OUT of the chair and it tipped over and hit the floor. She reached Austin's stiff back in two steps and reached out for his shoulder. He flinched when she squeezed it.

"I'm so sorry, Austin. I didn't mean to imply that it was your failure. You did everything you could, and you almost reached Dr. Fazal in time. I-if your commanding officers had sent you in sooner, I know you would've saved him—because you saved me."

He did a half turn, and her hand was pressed just above his thudding heart. She had the strongest desire to cup his hard jaw in her palm and ease the pain that flashed from his eyes.

He really had cared about Dr. Fazal, and he felt his loss almost as keenly as she did.

His thick, stubby lashes fell over his eyes as if to protect his private thoughts from her. "Okay, yeah. I know you didn't mean it that way."

She gave his chest a pat before stepping back. She usually liked keeping her distance from people, even men she was dating, but something about Austin Foley lured her in. It couldn't be because they had anything in common, because it sounded like he'd come from a wholesome background of family, fresh air and farm animals, and she'd come from…dysfunction, grime and animals of a different kind.

"Let's eat. You said you were starving, and now that I have my meeting with Patel, I've recovered my appetite. We can walk to the church from here."

"Maybe to do our initial surveillance followed by dinner, but when we go back for the meeting we have to drive."

"Why is that?"

"Because I'm not carrying a sniper rifle case along the Freedom Trail."

"Sniper rifle?"

"I'm going to cover you, Sophia, the best way I know how. If anyone gets near you…they're gone."

"What if they have the same idea and take me out before you even know they're in the area?"

"They're not going to take you out. They need you. They want to question you. They didn't need Ginny."

She puffed up her cheeks and blew out a breath. How could Austin get away with shooting someone on a Boston street corner? This would have to be covered up at a high level, but then it had taken high-level personnel to authorize a navy SEAL to operate stateside.

She had a feeling she didn't want to know any more.

"We can eat at Faneuil Hall—lots of choices there. We can walk or take the T from the church."

"I'll let you lead the way. Just as long as we're back at the hotel by nine o'clock, so I can get ready. Right now I'm going to shave and brush my teeth, unless you want to freshen up first." He stopped at the entrance to the bathroom.

"You go ahead. I'm going to make some phone calls to Anna and Morgan. Someone has to tell them about Ginny."

As Austin closed the bathroom door, she grabbed the framed picture of her and Dr. Fazal that she'd taken from the floor of his office and traced the crack on the glass that ran through his body. "I know you didn't want me to contact Patel, but Austin's here now—and he's going to make everything okay."

SOPHIA PUSHED AWAY her plate with her half-eaten meal and dug her elbows into the table. "Do you think you'll be able to see what's going on from the top of that building at night?"

"My scope has night vision." Austin aimed his fork at her plate. "Are you going to finish that fish?"

"Help yourself. I can't eat another bite."

"If you don't want to do this, you don't have to meet Patel. I'll meet him. If he clams up, I'll take him in. He's involved in whatever got Dr. Fazal killed, and our intelligence agencies have every right to question him."

"That doesn't mean he's going to talk to you." She took a sip of water. "He wants to talk to me. I'm sure he'll be more open with me, and then if you want to pick him up later, you can do so."

"Oh, I'm sure the FBI is going to want to pick him up later." He sawed off the edge of the salmon and popped it in his mouth. "You sure you don't want to eat the rest of this? You hardly touched your food."

"I'm too nervous to eat." Her gaze swept from his empty plate to her own, which he was in the process of emptying. "I guess nerves don't affect your appetite."

"I'm not nervous."

"You do this all the time?"

"In the middle of an American city? Uh, no." He signaled to the waitress. "Do you want dessert?"

"I'll have a bite of whatever you're having." She twisted the napkin in her lap. "So, this is a new experience for you, too, but you're not anxious about it."

"It's a job. It has to be done. I'm the one who has to do it."

He smiled at the approaching waitress as if they'd just been talking about the weather. "Can we get the caramel apple pie—and two forks?"

"Coming right up."

Five minutes later she watched Austin dig into that pie as if he wasn't going to be watching the Old North Church through the scope of a rifle.

Shoving the plate toward her, he said, "Try it."

She picked up her fork and then reached forward to dab a spot of caramel from his chin with the tip of her finger.

His eyes darkened for a moment to a murky, unfathomable green. She plunged her fork into a glob of ice cream.

"Make sure you get the apples, caramel and nuts."

The gooey sweetness exploded in her mouth and she closed her eyes and rolled her lips inward. "That's yummy. Can we just sit here, finish this delectable dessert and forget about Patel?"

"You can." He rested the tines of his fork on the edge of the plate. "I already told you, Sophia. I'll take care of this. The FBI will get info out of Patel—one way or the other."

"He wants to talk to me. If he'd wanted to bring US intelligence into this, he would've called you. I'm sure Dr. Fazal had you guys on speed dial."

"If he had, he didn't use it after making contact with Patel. Maybe if he'd called us first, we… I could've moved in sooner."

"There must be some reason he didn't after that first call, and I'm going to find out why tonight." She stuffed another piece of pie in her mouth before she could chicken out—besides, she had a navy SEAL sniper watching her back.

Austin paid the check, and if they weren't on their way to a meeting that could result in someone's death, this would've been a pretty damn good date—better than the Spark dates she'd been on.

When they hit the sidewalk, Austin stretched and said, "Let's take the T back to the hotel."

Yeah, because he had to get his rifle ready to shoot someone.

The short ride on the T brought them back to the hotel faster than she expected, faster than she wanted.

They got to the room, and Austin pulled a case that looked more secure than Fort Knox from the closet.

"If you didn't want to heighten the suspicions of the hotel staff—" she rapped her knuckles on the hard case "—I think you failed."

"I don't care if their suspicions are heightened. I just don't want them getting inside."

"What if they just hauled away the whole thing?"

"Impossible. It has a GPS tracker on it. They can give it a try though." He stuffed a black cap into his pocket. "Do you want to run through the plan once more?"

"We're going to park in the structure down the block, and then split up at the building on the corner. You're going to find your way to the roof of the building, and I'm going to keep walking toward the church. I'll come up from the right-hand side, and if I don't see Patel, with his baseball cap and scarf, I'll pace a few times in front of the church."

"What's the signal if you see anyone but Patel approaching you?"

"One if by land and two if by sea?"

"Funny. Tell me."

"I'm going to raise my scarf over my head, like this." She grabbed her scarf on either side and pulled it up toward her head.

"That's right."

"And you're going to take out the interloper."

"Take him out as in kill him? No. Let's just say I'll make him think twice before approaching you."

"Where were you during my formative years?"

"If I'd have known you and known you needed protection? I would've delivered."

He'd made the pronouncement with a half smile on his face, but she believed him.

"Are you the eldest of the three brothers and two sisters?"

He nodded as he hoisted the case from the bed.

"You must've protected them, too—scared the stuffing out of your sisters' boyfriends and put the bullies in place who were picking on your brothers."

Her words had wiped the smile from his face, casting a shadow over his features. He shrugged. "I never cared who my sisters dated."

She'd said something wrong but didn't know what. She was supposed to be the complicated one. "Okay, then. Let's do this."

She picked up the framed photo again, and this time a piece of glass fell out and hit the carpet. "I'm going to get a new frame for this."

"Where was that taken?" Austin leaned over her shoulder.

"It was at a conference in Chicago, where I won an award. H-he was so proud of me. Nobody has ever been proud of me like that, and I doubt ever will again."

He took the frame from her hands and placed it on the credenza. "Don't sell yourself short,

Sophia. You're about to do something pretty amazing right now."

"I just hope Peter Patel has some answers."

As they walked through the hotel, only a few people gave Austin's case a second glance. Probably thought he was the trombone player for the Boston Pops.

When they got to his rental car in the hotel parking lot, Austin did a thorough search of the vehicle. They drove to the church in silence.

Sophia couldn't stop her leg from bouncing, so she settled for closing her eyes and taking deep breaths. She didn't want to meet Patel only to faint at his feet.

Austin found parking on the first floor of the structure and retrieved his weapon from the trunk of the car.

"Remember, if anything happens, you take off running back to the car—unless you're being followed. Then you run toward the street and the most populated area you can find."

"Got it." She saluted, but she felt like throwing up.

He must've seen the look before because he cupped her face with one hand. "I'll be watching you. I'll keep you safe."

"I know." She'd never been surer of anything in her life.

He held her hand as they left the structure and

as they strolled down the sidewalk just like any other couple on a date.

Then he gave her fingers a squeeze and slipped into the building where he'd be watching her from the roof.

Loosening her scarf around her neck, she followed the red line on the sidewalk that marked the Freedom Trail, traversed by millions of tourists every year.

The white walls of the Old North Church gleamed in the darkness and she focused on the beacon of light the church represented. Nothing would happen to her here, not at Dr. Fazal's favorite place in all of Boston.

He'd loved the story of Paul Revere and his midnight ride. He respected rebels. He'd been one himself.

A couple walked toward her and veered left toward the square. Sophia let out a sigh and then sucked it back in when she saw a lone figure in a baseball cap sitting on a bench under the trees across from the church's entrance. Was his scarf red?

The lights around the church didn't extend that far, so she squinted into the darkness. Should she call out? He hadn't seemed to notice her—hadn't made a move.

Sophia glanced over her shoulder. Several feet behind her, two women walked up to the gate surrounding the church and peered through the bars. Then they wandered toward the street.

Sophia straightened her spine and marched toward Patel, who hadn't yet lifted his head. Did he want her to identify herself?

"Mr. Patel?" She slowed her steps.

He didn't budge.

She swiped her tongue across her dry lips. "Mr. Patel?"

She got within five feet of the bench when the smell hit her full force—the same odor from Dr. Fazal's office, the same odor from that nightmarish afternoon when she was four years old.

She gagged and stumbled forward, falling to her knees in front of Patel.

Then she noticed it—blood dripping from his neck, soaking his red scarf, pooling beneath the bench.

So. Much. Blood.

Chapter Nine

Austin's pulse flickered in his throat. What was she doing?

Through his scope, he saw Sophia crouch in front of the figure on the bench. Were they talking? The man, Patel, still had his head down, his chin practically resting on his chest.

Sophia now blocked his view of Patel's body, but it looked like she'd taken his hand in hers. What the hell was going on?

He did a quick sweep of the surrounding area. The couple who'd strolled into the quad was still sitting there, their backs to Sophia and Patel. After the two women who'd peeked in at the church, nobody else had come along.

He brought Sophia and Patel back into focus. She cranked her head over her shoulder. His heart skipped a beat and he sucked in a breath.

Something had gone wrong.

His muscles tensed as he got ready to push

off the wall. Then another figure came into his sights. A man had come around the corner, moving at a brisk clip, his hand in his pocket, his focus on Sophia.

Austin got the man in his crosshairs, and then he adjusted his aim downward and fired off a shot. The cement post in front of the man exploded.

The stranger jumped back, his head twisting from side to side.

Austin muttered under his breath, "You're not getting anywhere near her, you SOB."

He squeezed the trigger again and another cement post shattered into pieces. One of them must've hit the guy, because he jerked like a puppet and grabbed his leg.

Sophia lurched to her feet and Austin silently yelled at her to run. She must've heard him.

As the man stumbled back and the couple in the square jumped to their feet, Sophia took off. Patel remained on the bench, and Austin could now see a dark stain spreading across his front.

The stranger had taken one step toward Sophia's retreating figure and then thought better of it. He spun around and limped off in the other direction.

Austin could no longer see Sophia and just hoped to hell she was heading back to the car in the lot. He kept watch for several more seconds.

The couple had approached Patel. They both sprang back at the same instant. The man got on his cell phone, and there was nothing more Austin could do.

He pushed away from his station, slinging the case over his shoulder, where it banged against his hip as he ran toward the staircase. He broke down his rifle at full speed while he negotiated the steps.

By the time he reached the bottom of the building, his rifle was in pieces. He leaned against the door to the street and stashed the parts back in the case. Then he pushed out onto the sidewalk and strode toward the parking structure.

He found himself chanting Sophia's name like some magical incantation—as if that would be enough to make her appear beside the car. The sirens in the distance quickened his pace.

His bullets were untraceable, and if Patel had been shot, there would be no match between his bullets and the ones that had killed Patel. Who knew what the cops would make of it?

Had the couple in the square noticed Sophia? Would they be able to provide some kind of description of her to the Boston PD? It didn't matter. The FBI could get her out of anything at this point—if they wanted to.

With his breath coming hard and fast, he

turned into the parking structure. He zeroed in on his rental and his gut knotted. No Sophia.

He pressed the key fob and the car's lights flashed once. A head poked out from the post beside the car and relief swept through his body.

He called out to Sophia, "Hop in."

He opened the trunk and hoisted his weapon inside. When he slid into the driver's seat, he reached across the console and took Sophia's face in both of his hands and landed a hard kiss on her mouth.

"God, I'm glad to see you."

"Same." She snapped her seat belt, which suddenly hit him as ridiculous after what she'd just been through.

He laughed, and she scowled at him.

"What happened to that man you shot at? You missed him."

"I missed him on purpose. There are just so many dead bodies we can leave on the streets of Boston. Besides, I didn't see a weapon on him. I'm not authorized to commit murder." He threw the car in Reverse and the tires squealed on the polished cement as he wheeled out of the structure. "He took off in the other direction from you. I guess he didn't want to take his chances on where the next bullet would land."

"I didn't even notice him coming up on me until you took the shot."

"What happened to Patel? I didn't see that he was dead until you'd moved away from him."

"Someone slit his throat." She squeezed her eyes shut as if trying to erase the image from her vision.

"I'm sorry you had to see that." He checked his rearview mirror as he pulled up to the intersection. An ambulance flew past him. "They probably followed him or were able to track him. Even if they hacked into his phone, they wouldn't know Dr. Fazal's favorite place in Boston."

She hugged herself, and he wished it were his arms wrapped around her body.

She tipped her head to the side, resting against the window. "I guess the one silver lining to this is that Dr. Fazal's killers aren't out to kill me."

"Yet."

Her body twitched and he clamped down on his bottom lip. He didn't want to blacken the one bright spot she'd been holding on to, but he did want her to face reality and get rid of the crazy idea that if she opened up to these guys they'd believe that she didn't know anything about Patel and Fazal and let her go about her business.

They'd never allow that.

"One thing they do know now…"

"What's that?" He glanced at her profile.

"If they believed I was with some random boyfriend the other night in Cambridge who'd gotten lucky and disarmed a man with a gun, those crazy shots from nowhere just disabused them of that notion."

"You're right." He lifted his shoulders. "And that's not a bad thing."

"Will it make them give up?"

"Probably not, but it might make them more desperate and that might make them more careless, and that's not a bad thing either."

They returned to the hotel and he hauled his weapon case from the trunk. Fewer people were milling around the hotel now than when they'd left, and nobody gave his strange case a second glance.

When they got to the room, he locked the rifle up again and stored it upright in the back of the closet. He grabbed two bottles of water from the minifridge and tossed one to Sophia, who'd stretched out on the bed and kicked off her boots.

He dragged a chair to the foot of the bed and slumped in it, facing her. "I wonder how they got around Patel to…to kill him."

"I don't know. I wonder how long he'd been on that bench before I arrived."

"I guess all we really know is that they followed him and didn't want him communicating any information to you. Also, the fact that they killed him indicates to me that they didn't need any info from him...or they'd already gotten it."

She dragged a pillow into her lap and punched it. "I was hoping we'd get some answers tonight."

"We don't even know who Patel is—was. That, at least, would have helped."

Gasping, she rolled off the bed and lunged for her purse. "We can find out."

He eyed the phone she had pinched between two fingers. "Did you take his picture?"

"God, no, but this is even better." She dangled the phone in the air. "I got his fingerprints."

"What?"

"When I realized he was dead and that he wouldn't be telling me anything about why he came into Dr. Fazal's life, I got so frustrated. Crazy angry at him. I took out my phone and curled his hand around it."

"*That's* what you were doing." He smacked his forehead with the heel of his hand. "I thought you were holding his hand or something. I couldn't figure out what was going on. How in the hell did you have the presence of mind to do that?"

"Presence of mind? I felt like I was losing my

mind. I didn't even remember I'd done it until you talked about not knowing his identity."

"You did do it, and I think that's amazing. I'm impressed." He shook out a napkin from the coffee area and placed it on the table by the window. "Put it here."

"Can you lift the prints from the phone?"

"Me personally? No, but the local FBI office can do it for me. I'll contact them tomorrow, and we can find out who Patel is and his connection to Dr. Fazal." Austin circled his finger over the phone. "Where are his prints?"

"I pressed the pads of his fingertips against the screen at the top. I've just handled the phone by the edges and haven't touched it since I brought it out just now. Will that work?"

"Not only will it work, it's brilliant. Really quick thinking on your part."

"Like I said, it was more like I was on autopilot." She coughed. "As you've probably figured out from researching my background, I've had a lot of contact with the police over the years."

"I don't know as much about you as you seem to think, but from what I do know, if you had a lot of contact with law enforcement it wasn't your fault."

She wedged her hands on her hips and tilted her head. "You don't strike me as the type of person who would make excuses for someone's bad behavior."

Usually he wasn't, but his impression of Sophia had done a one-eighty since he'd met her and spent some time with her.

"Some excuses carry more weight than others." Shoving his hands into his pockets, he braced a shoulder against the window. "Do you remember much…about your father's death?"

She blinked, and her face tightened.

For a minute he thought she was going to tell him to go to hell, and maybe he deserved that for prying. Had anyone but the therapists ever asked her about that afternoon when she was four years old?

"Interesting that you should ask that now." She caught a strand of her dark hair and twisted it around one finger. "When I smelled the blood pooling around Patel, and before, when I smelled it in Dr. Fazal's office, it reminded me of that day more than anything."

"I've heard smell is one of the strongest triggers for memory, so that makes sense."

"Yeah, except for most people it's the smell of apple pie and Mom's old perfume that tweak those memories." She flipped her hair over her shoulder. "I was in the bedroom when my parents started arguing."

"Was your father abusive? I know your mother didn't get off on self-defense because, well…"

"Yeah, she's still in prison." Sophia dropped onto the bed and fell backward. She continued as she stared at the ceiling. "My father wasn't abusive, unless you call it abuse when a drug pusher yells at his wife for using his product."

His hands curled into fists. Her father *was* abusive—abusive for creating that kind of world for a child. "Is that what they were arguing about?"

"Yes, but this time he miscalculated. My mom was already high…and desperate for more. When he denied her and called her a junkie, it was the last straw. She grabbed his gun, which he kept handy for drug deals, and shot him twice. Then she had all the crank she wanted. I'm sure she would've OD'd if a neighbor in the apartment next door hadn't called 911 when she heard the gunshots."

"Is that when you came out of the bedroom?"

"He was lying on the kitchen floor. My mother didn't even try to keep me away from him. The first cops on the scene told me I had blood on my dirty bare feet." Sophia spoke in a monotone, as if she were recounting the plot of a TV show and not her life.

He joined her on the bed, sitting on the edge. "God, I don't even know what to say. How you got to the point in your life where you are now after a beginning like that is a testament to your fortitude and spirit."

She rolled her eyes to the side, catching him with her gaze. "I had a lot of speed bumps on the way—running away from foster homes, fights, shoplifting—but not drugs, never drugs."

"Do you ever see your mother?"

"She's only about twenty-five miles away in Framingham."

"That means you do see her?"

"Once in a while. She's clean, remorseful, got her GED and found God."

"Sounds like progress." He toed off his running shoes and stacked a few pillows against the headboard. "Is she getting out anytime soon?"

"She got twenty-five to life. She's coming up for parole soon."

"Will you be there for her?"

"Was she there for me?"

"No." He eased back against the pillows. "I'm not implying you should let her into your life. Just asking."

She slid from the bed and grabbed the remote. "Do you think there's anything on the nightly news about Patel's murder?"

"It's past eleven. If the local news had the story, we probably missed it."

Sophia clicked on the TV anyway, probably to get away from his probing questions.

The Boston-area news had already switched from hard news stories to the warm and fuzzy human-interest ones—and there was nothing warm or fuzzy about a man getting his throat sliced on a bench across from the Old North Church.

Austin yawned. "I'm going to wrap it up. Once I get the go-ahead to bring your phone in for dusting, I'll take it to the office, and if the FBI can't find a match in the national database, the prints can be sent to Interpol—thanks to you."

"Do you think they'll give me a medal?"

"I think I can arrange for that." He winked at her.

"Actually, all I want is to be safe in my own apartment again."

"I think I can arrange for that, too."

She placed the remote next to the TV and started pulling cushions from the sofa bed. "Do you think the Boston PD will be able to identify Patel from his fingerprints?"

"Not if he's a foreigner. If they can't ID him, they'll send his prints to the FBI, anyway. We'll just get the information faster this way. Like I said before, my operation is not going through the normal channels."

"But you think the FBI will take the prints from the phone, anyway?"

"Someone there will receive special orders to do so."

"I always figured there was a conspiracy between law enforcement agencies that went completely over the general public's head. In a way, I feel vindicated."

"The general public probably doesn't want to know what's going on." He jumped up to help her pull out the sofa bed. "I don't know why you're getting this bed ready. This is mine."

"This is your room and you're quite a bit bigger than I am, so you should get that comfy king-size bed."

"Shucks, ma'am. That wouldn't be the chivalrous thing to do."

"Hey, if you insist. You don't have to twist my arm." She turned from the sofa bed and opened her suitcase, emerging with a bag dangling from her fingertips. "Can I have the bathroom first, too?"

"Of course. I'll get my bed ready."

"I'm kinda liking this chivalry thing." She swept past him and clicked the bathroom door behind her.

Clenching his jaw, he pulled out the couch and smoothed his hands across the sheets. If she could read his real thoughts on the matter, she'd rethink everything about him.

Because he wanted nothing more than to lay Sophia across that king-size bed and explore every inch of her body—with his tongue.

What would she think about his chivalry then?

Chapter Ten

The following morning, Sophia emerged from a sound sleep, one twitching muscle and one thought at a time. With her body fully stretched out and her mind fully aware of last night's horrific events, she lifted her head to peer at Austin splayed out on the sofa bed.

A tickle of guilt played out across the back of her neck as she eyed Austin on his stomach, his leg hanging off the side of the bed, his arm flung over his head and the sheets tangled about his body as if he'd been wrestling with them all night. He probably had.

She scooched up to a sitting position, her eyes gradually becoming accustomed to the gloom of the room. With the sheets shrugged from his broad shoulders and twisted around his waist, he looked like a Greek god who'd fallen to Earth for a nap between battles.

On her hands and knees, she crawled to the

end of the bed to get a better look, and got an eyeful of his smooth, bare back, strong enough to carry the weight of the world's safety—or at least her own.

He cleared his throat and thrashed his legs, the sheet bunching and scooting farther down his back.

She released a small sigh when she saw the edge of his black briefs. Not that she was hoping for a glimpse of his bare backside, but it would've considerably brightened her morning after a bad night in a series of bad nights.

Her gaze traveled from his buttocks, teasingly concealed by the sheet, over his smooth back and across those muscled shoulders until it collided with a pair of green eyes. She couldn't see their greenness in the dim light, but she knew the color by now. She'd gotten lost in that color a few times.

The heat surged in her cheeks, but he wouldn't be able to see the blush any more than she could see the color of his eyes. "Oh, are you awake? I—I thought I heard your phone go off."

"My phone's over there." He rolled onto his back and flung his arm out to the side. "Are you okay?"

"I'm fine. Why?"

"Isn't it early?"

She twisted around to see the glowing numbers of the alarm clock. "It's seven twenty. Is that early?"

"I guess not." He rubbed his eyes. "It's so dark in here."

"Those drapes do a pretty good job of shutting out the light, and I think we're facing west."

Closing his eyes, he made a halfhearted kick at the sheets wound around his legs. "Seems earlier."

"I'm sorry. You didn't have a very good night's sleep, did you? Bed's too small for you."

"That's not why. I can sleep in any condition, and have. This sofa bed is heaven compared to some of the mattresses I've endured—and some of the rock ledges that have doubled as mattresses."

She held her breath waiting for him to explain why he'd had a restless night. Could it have been because she was in the bed two feet away from him? No. A man like him? A woman like her? Just no.

"Did you sleep well?"

"I was exhausted. I don't think I slept so much as passed out." She jerked her thumb over her shoulder. "Do you want the shower first since I had first dibs last night?"

"You go ahead." His legs finally free of the

sheets, he stretched and all the muscles in his body rippled. "I'm going to make a few phone calls and see where we can take your cell to get those prints."

She peeled her tongue from the roof of her dry mouth. She really wanted to hang around to see him in his briefs, but she didn't want to be too obvious, so she crawled out of the bed and shuffled to her suitcase.

As she crouched beside her bag, she tugged at the hem of her T-shirt. She really needed to buy herself some new pajamas.

She dug through her clean clothes and pulled out a pair of black leggings and an oversize sweater. At least it had a wide neckline that exposed one shoulder, so she wouldn't be completely lacking in sex appeal.

She hugged a camisole to her chest and shook her head. Sex appeal wasn't required for submitting the fingerprints of a dead man. Had she lost all perspective?

A soft noise behind her caught her attention and she cranked her head over her shoulder. Her eyes widened and her pulse throbbed as she took in the sight of Austin strolling to the window in nothing but his black briefs. Right now, this was the only perspective she wanted.

Before he could catch her checking him out

again, she staggered to her feet, her clothes bunched in her arms, and scurried to the bathroom.

Once in the shower, she got a grip and returned to reality. She and Austin were in a bubble right now—a bubble of fear and uncertainty. Other than Dr. Fazal, she'd never had a protective male figure in her life. She had to separate her emotional connection and dependence on Austin from the real reason he was acting as her guardian.

He had a job to do, and once the CIA or whoever was pulling his strings had decided he'd done as much as they needed, they'd yank him off the case and send him back overseas.

She had to prepare for that eventuality and stop having ridiculous thoughts about him— and his body. She still had Tyler Cannon, her Spark date, waiting for her, and maybe a few more connections to check out once she was able to use her phone again.

She finished her shower with her feet on the ground and her head out of the clouds. After towel drying her hair and pulling her black camisole over her head, she tucked her sweater under her arm. Forget the sex appeal.

She marched back into the room, her glance sweeping past Austin, entering a text in his phone. At least he'd had the decency to cover all those flexing muscles with a white T-shirt and his jeans from last night.

He looked up from his phone. "Wow, I bet you look good in that red color."

"This?" She held up the sweater she'd been ready to dump back into her suitcase. "Yeah, I like red."

She stuffed her arms into the sweater and yanked it over her head. It was a just a sweater, not a shimmering cocktail dress.

"I made contact." He held up his phone. "The CIA's sending me to a guy, Melvin, in the Massachusetts Department of Justice. He'll lift the prints and send them to the FBI first for a check against the national database. If there's no match there, he has a connection to Interpol and we can see if we can get a fingerprint database from Pakistan."

"That sounds like a long shot. Does Pakistan even have a database with fingerprints?"

"I don't have a clue. That's not our area."

"What are the police going to find when they search for Patel's identity?"

"I don't know. Maybe he'll have fake ID. What I do know is that I've already contacted the agency that's running the show out here and indicated that I need to get into Patel's homicide file."

"They can do that?"

"They have computer guys—and one amazing woman—who can hack into anything."

"Who is *they*, Austin? Who's calling the shots for you other than the navy?"

"I can't tell you that, Sophia."

"Would anyone, including me, even know this organization?"

"No." He slid open the closet door and pulled some clothes from a few hangers. "We'll get going as soon as I'm done."

"Take your time." She parked herself in front of the full-length mirror on the closet door and ran her hands through her damp hair.

She caught his eye in the mirror. "What?"

"You *do* look good in that color."

He slammed the bathroom door, and she smiled at her reflection in the mirror—a big, silly grin that spelled trouble.

WITH HER CELL phone back in her possession and clutched in her hand, Sophia took the seat across from Austin in a small breakfast café across the street from the Commons. "Do you really think Melvin will have an answer on those prints at the end of the day?"

"It's a rush order, and Melvin seems like a competent guy." Austin shook open the plastic menu. "He'll get to the national database, anyway. It's going to take longer for Interpol to get back to him—even with the CIA pressuring them."

She turned her coffee cup upright and smiled at the waiter. When he'd filled her cup and Austin's, Sophia continued. "The CIA knows about your assignment, but you're not reporting primarily to them, are you? The CIA is not calling the shots here."

"Why are you so interested?" He peered at her over the top of his menu, wiggling his eyebrows up and down.

"It fascinates me—the dark, twisting corridors of power."

"You make it sound...nefarious. It's all done to protect people like you—" he tipped his menu toward the other tables "—and the people in this restaurant, and the people waiting for their tours to begin in Boston Commons."

She rolled her eyes. "If you say so."

He hunched forward, opened his mouth and then must've thought better of it. "I think I'm going to have the pancakes. You?"

"I'm not a breakfast person." She cradled her coffee cup with two hands. "Maybe some toast."

As they gave their order to the waiter, Austin's phone vibrated on the table. He ignored it until their waiter left, and then he grabbed it.

"Not the fingerprints yet."

He shook his head. "Almost better. The initial police report on Patel's murder."

"Are they still calling him Peter Patel?"

"They are." He swept his fingertip across his phone's display. "Which means he must've been carrying fake ID."

"Have they made any connection between him and Dr. Fazal?"

"Not that I can see, but when we get back to the hotel I'll bring the report up on my laptop." He placed the phone beside his coffee cup and tapped the screen twice. "I got what I wanted right now though."

"What's that?"

"The hotel where he was staying."

"Have the police been there yet?"

"I'm sure they have, but it doesn't mean I can't check it out."

"We. *We* can check it out. I'm not sitting around in that hotel waiting for you. Besides..." She dropped her lashes and ran the tip of her finger along the rim of her cup. "I—I just feel safer when I'm with you."

When she looked at him through her lowered lashes, she caught her breath. His raised eyebrows told her he wasn't buying her "poor pitiful me" act.

"You'd be perfectly safe in that hotel room, especially since you're packing your own heat.

You want to come along because you want to be in on the action—you want to be proactive in getting justice for Dr. Fazal. I get it."

The waiter arrived with a stack of blueberry pancakes for Austin and some rye toast for her. "Anything else I can get you?"

They both declined, and Austin dumped a pile of whipped butter on top of his pancakes.

"You don't have to use tricks with me, Sophia. You don't have to pretend to be someone you're not—because I like you, as is."

She watched him dig into his pancakes through narrowed eyes. He didn't want to take care of the soft, helpless woman? She'd rarely been soft or helpless in her life, but she could've given it a try—for Austin.

Back at the hotel an hour later, Austin brought up the police report on Patel's homicide on his laptop and scrolled through it. Patel had died, bled out, probably moments before Sophia discovered him. Thank God Patel's killer hadn't ambushed Sophia before Austin had him in his crosshairs.

There were no akas listed in Patel's file, so as far as the Boston PD was concerned, the murder victim was Peter Patel, a visitor to Boston from California and staying at the Cambridge Arms Hotel—even his room number was listed in the report. Money and credit cards had been lifted from Patel's wallet to make it look like a robbery. Of course, the cops had to be thinking, what street criminal would slit a man's throat to get cash and credit cards?

"What did you find out? Where was he staying?" Sophia sat on the bed beside him, crossing her legs beneath her.

His gaze glanced across her creamy shoulder where her sweater dropped off and then meandered to her dark eyes, sparkling with interest and intelligence. He preferred this engaged presence to the scared female persona she felt she had to employ to convince him to take her with him when he went to Patel's hotel room. Did she really believe he wanted a damsel in distress? Did he? Had he?

If he examined the truth head-on, most of the women he'd dated back home had been softer, more domesticated, more interested in a diamond on their left hand than one piercing the side of their nose.

"Hotel?" She cocked her head and her inky hair fanned across her exposed shoulder.

"The Cambridge Arms. Know it?"

"Nope. Sounds like one of those places thrown up to accommodate the parents of all those college students." She tugged on her earlobe. "The cops think this is a robbery?"

"Uh–huh. His killer even stole money and credit cards from his wallet."

"Oh, and just decided to slice him from ear to ear after they got their eighty bucks?"

"I'm sure that's under their consideration."

"When do we head over to the Cambridge Arms and what are we going to find? The cops have probably already been there, right?"

"I'm sure they have. They probably even removed some items from the room if they thought something had particular significance."

"Will we find anything left that could help us?"

"We might. I'm not going to pass up the chance to find out."

Her cell phone buzzed and she leaned forward to snatch it from the bedside table. Her fingers played across the display as she made a slight turn away from him.

Austin ground his back teeth, and he tapped his keyboard a little harder than he had to. When he'd had possession of her cell, he couldn't help noticing a few more messages rolling in from that dating app. Was that what she was doing now? Answering her so-called dates?

He sniffed. Was that the kind of guy she wanted? Someone who spent time trolling for women online instead of meeting them face-to-face?

He rubbed his hand across his mouth. And how exactly was that any of his business?

She cupped her phone in her palm. "When are we going to Cambridge?"

"As soon as I finish going through this report."

"You don't think we should wait until nighttime?"

"Less conspicuous during the day, and we don't have to worry about turning on any lights in his room—in case someone's watching."

Dragging her bottom lip between her teeth, she tossed her phone from hand to hand. "Do you think his killers know where he was staying?"

"They went through his pockets to take money from his wallet, so they saw his hotel key. They know."

"So, they might be there?"

"Which is another reason why we're going in the daylight. They know the police have been or will be in Cambridge. They'll wait until they think it's safe."

"What if the police catch us?"

"You forget." He thumped his chest once. "Even though I'm supposed to be under law enforcement's radar, if worse comes to worse and they make me, I have an out."

"It would cause some kind of…incident

though, wouldn't it? A US Navy SEAL involved in an operation in the homeland."

"It would be a problem—but I don't intend to get caught."

"Oh, I won't get caught either." She flicked back her dark hair. "I got away with plenty back in the day."

"I'll bet you still do."

A pretty pink tinged her cheeks, and then she rolled off the bed. "I'll let you finish so we can get going. Something to drink from the vending machine?"

"I still have a water in the fridge."

"I need...something."

She banged out of the room, and Austin eased back against the stack of pillows. Despite the electricity between them, Sophia wasn't comfortable with flirtation—and he needed to stop flirting with her and stop thinking about what she was and was not comfortable with. He needed to protect her against Fazal's killers and that was it.

After the identification of Patel, he could be out of here and on the first plane back to Somalia. He and his team of snipers still had plenty of unfinished business with a nasty terrorist with the code name Vlad.

By the time Sophia had returned to the room, he'd gone through the rest of the police file and was stuffing his feet into his running shoes. "Did you get lost on the way to the soda machine across the hall?"

"I decided to take a quick look around the hotel. There's an indoor pool and Jacuzzi on the first floor."

"Yeah, this would be a great spot…if I was on vacation." He grabbed his jacket. "Are you ready?"

"Do you have a plan?"

He winked at her. "I always have a plan."

Except for a plan to deal with his attraction to a woman he'd just met and might have to leave just as quickly.

The drive over the bridge and into Cambridge didn't take long, and Sophia seemed preoccupied with her own thoughts. She'd been through a helluva few days. Before this craziness she probably thought she'd seen her lifetime quota of dead bodies after her mother killed her father.

She'd needed to catch a break, and she'd gotten that break when Dr. Hamid Fazal came into her life. After losing his own wife and daughters, Fazal had probably taken Sophia under his wing without hesitation. Sophia would've trusted someone like Fazal immediately, given their shared losses.

Did she trust him? Most women did, but Sophia wasn't most women.

He spotted the Cambridge Arms and then circled the block. "I don't want to park in the hotel lot. We might need to be guests, anyway, and I don't want to draw attention."

"You'll never find a parking place on the street, but there's a public lot around the corner."

"I know how much you object to paying for parking, so I'll get it. All my expenses are re-imbursable."

"The navy's going to be wondering why you shelled out so much for parking."

He rolled his eyes and made a U-turn into a public lot.

As they walked across the street, Sophia asked, "What's the plan?"

"I'm sure most of the hotel employees are aware that one of their guests was murdered. Even if they aren't, the police most likely left instructions to keep Patel's room off-limits."

"That's not very encouraging."

"But—" he held up his index finger "—most hotels have a master card key that opens all the rooms, and we're going to snag one of those."

"*You're* going to snag one of those." She poked his arm. "I promised Dr. Fazal my life of crime was over."

"Don't worry."

Getting the master proved easier than he expected, and he didn't even have to plan the disturbance down the hall that took the hotel maid's attention away from her cart. With the card in his jacket pocket, he led Sophia to the stairwell and up two flights to Patel's room.

The maids had already finished or hadn't started on this floor yet, which made their break-in easier. With his gloves still on, he slid the key home and pushed open the door, giving Sophia a nudge in ahead of him.

He caught the door before it slammed and eased it closed as he scanned the room. He flipped the inside lock. "Cops already did a number in here."

Sophia had pulled on her own gloves and circled the room, hands on her hips. "Where do we start and what are we looking for?"

"Any personal effects—pictures, postcards, letters. Examine every piece of paper you come across for names, addresses and places."

"Would the cops have already taken that stuff?"

"I'm sure they did. It is a murder investigation, and they need to contact the next of kin."

"Wherever they are."

"Probably Pakistan."

Sophia blew out a breath and rolled her shoulders. "Okay, I'll start with his suitcases."

Austin strode to the nightstand and opened the drawers, looking for papers and anything jotted down on the hotel menu or flyers. He even thumbed through the Bible.

"Nothing but clothes in here." Sophia flipped down the cover of one suitcase. "I'll check the side pockets."

He moved to the bathroom, hoping to find a leftover prescription bottle.

Sophia called from the other room, "Patel sure read a lot of different newspapers."

"Anything written on them?" He poked his head out of the bathroom when he heard a clicking noise at the hotel door. Never breaking contact with Sophia's wide eyes, he held a finger to his lips.

He crept from the bathroom and flattened himself against the wall behind the door. It opened slowly and then halted against the inside lock he'd flipped into place earlier.

Someone on the other side of that door sucked in a sharp breath.

Austin glanced at Sophia, who was still crouched on the floor next to Patel's suitcase, an armful of newspapers clutched to her chest.

Sidling along the wall, Austin made his way to Sophia and then grabbed her arm, pulling her to her feet. He pointed at the sliding glass door that led to a small balcony.

She shook her head and breathed into his ear, "We're three floors up."

She didn't have to tell him that, but whoever was outside that door wasn't leaving until they did, and soon there might be someone stationed outside, as well.

He took two steps toward the door and tugged at it. It opened on a whisper. When Sophia joined him on the balcony, he closed the door behind them and peered over the railing around the edge.

Turning toward him, Sophia grabbed his jacket. "I can't do this."

"Sure you can." He chucked her under the chin. "There's a balcony beneath this one. If we hang off the edge, we can reach it by swinging our legs and jumping onto it. We should be able to drop to those bushes below from the second floor."

"I—I'm afraid of heights. I can't."

He cupped her face in his hands. "You do it, or we have some kind of gun battle with the people trying to get into this room. I'll go first, and I'll catch you. Do you trust me?"

If she didn't want to do it, he'd go to battle for her, but he hoped she trusted him enough to take a chance.

Could she take a chance on him?

Chapter Eleven

Sophia swallowed. Her gaze drifted past Austin's shoulder to the hotel door, which had closed—for now. Who was on the other side? If it were the cops, they would've said something.

She focused on Austin's face, strong, confident. Did she trust him? More than anything else in her life right now.

She released a breath. "Tell me what to do."

Smoothing his gloved thumbs across her cheeks, he said, "You got this, but we're gonna have to hurry."

To make his point, Austin gave her a little shove from behind toward the railing that separated her from thirty feet to sudden death.

"Watch me."

Gripping the top of the railing he flung his body over the ledge. Sophia watched him slide his hands to the bottom rung of the railing and swing like he was competing in a gymnastics event.

She'd always been really, really bad at gymnastics.

When Austin disappeared below her, she clutched her suddenly tight throat. His voice floated up from beneath her. "Your turn. Hoist yourself over and scoot your hands as far down as you can."

Licking her lips, she glanced over her shoulder into the room. Had the door opened again?

She curled her hands around the railing and swung one leg over. She perched there like a giant awkward bird for a few seconds before rolling her body into oblivion. She squeaked once as her legs dangled in midair.

Austin's hand stroked her ankle. "Ready to swing?"

She began to work her shoulder muscles to propel her hips forward. She kicked her legs to increase her momentum just like when she was a kid on the swing set in the run-down park that was her refuge. She closed her eyes and swung harder. If she ever needed to escape, this was it.

"You're doing great. I'm going to tell you when to release and you're just going to let go."

Let go? Right.

But when Austin gave his command, she released. His strong arms wrapped around her legs and yanked her into the balcony below.

Her body flew into his and he stumbled back, taking her with him.

They landed with a thump and a crash into the metal chair stationed on the balcony.

Her eyes flew open and she looked into his face, meeting his slightly amused green gaze.

"That wasn't so hard, was it?"

With her body stretched out on top of his, their faces inches away from each other's, she'd never felt better. She rested her head against his shoulder. "That was crazy. Now you're telling me we need to jump off this balcony two stories high into those bushes down there?"

"We're in luck." He tipped his head back. "The guests in this room left their slider unlocked."

Raising her head, she squinted through the window. "They're not in there, are they?"

"I'm pretty sure they would've come running out here if they were." He shifted beneath her and grunted. "Are we going to stay out here all afternoon, or would you like to get going?"

She wouldn't mind lying on top of him for the rest of the day, but they had a killer or killers waiting for them.

She rolled off his body and onto her knees.

"We'd better hurry before the people in this room come back."

Austin scrambled to his feet and pulled open the door, poking his head inside the room. "I think our luck is holding. Doesn't look like anyone's staying here."

She squeezed past him into the room, taking a deep breath of his masculine scent. She'd never forget it. If the tinny smell of blood would always remind her of her father's death, this woodsy scent would always bring Austin back into her thoughts.

They crossed the room and Austin tucked her behind him when they got to the door. "Hang on."

He peeked out the peephole and then eased open the door. "Let's head for the stairwell. I have my gun ready in my pocket. If I tell you to duck…duck."

"You got me this far. I'll be the best damned soldier you ever encountered."

He squeezed the back of her neck. "You already are."

When the fresh air hit her face and whipped her hair into tangles, Sophia almost collapsed from the relief.

Sensing her frailty, Austin took her arm and hustled her down the sidewalk. "Let's keep moving. We're almost to the car."

He wasted no time once they were buckled in throwing the car into gear and peeling out of the parking lot. He smacked the steering wheel with the heel of his hand. "All that risk for nothing. The police left nothing behind—if Patel even left any clues in the room."

"I did take these." Sophia tugged at the zipper on her jacket and pulled out a bunch of newspapers.

"What the hell? How did you manage that?"

"I had just found them when someone tried the door. You'd told me to check for writing, but I didn't have time so I just zipped them up in my jacket. I thought I might lose them when I was swinging from the side of the hotel, but the bottom hem of my jacket is fitted and they stayed put. They may've even helped break my fall when I landed on top of you."

"For you, maybe."

"Did I hurt you?"

"You couldn't hurt me if you tried, but I did get nailed with the chair leg."

Could the same be said for her? Not that he would ever hurt her on purpose, but this flirtatious game he was playing with her could only end badly.

"Now that I have the newspapers, let me take a look to see if he wrote anything on them." She smoothed out the papers on her lap and flipped over each page, her gaze scanning the black-and-white print.

"There's nothing out of the ordinary here." She tucked the first paper under the other two and skimmed through the next one, and then the next. She slumped in the seat and sighed. "Nothing."

"Let's get some lunch." He drummed his thumbs on the steering wheel. "I'm driving in the opposite direction of Boston. Anywhere you want to go?"

"How can you think about food after the day we just had?"

"Look at it this way—you never know when you're going to need energy to jump out of windows and swing from balconies." He patted his flat belly. "I need sustenance."

"I hope that's the last jump I take from a window for a while." She looked out the window and studied the road signs. "Lexington. It's less than an hour away."

"Lead the way."

She gave him directions to a small lunch place with some booths for privacy. She didn't know what Austin's next move was going to be and maybe he didn't either, but they needed some time to figure it out—unless his shadowy superiors had already figured it out for him.

He parked the car down the street from the

restaurant and ducked his head to read the street sign out the window. "We're near the Lexington Battle Green."

"Haven't you ever played tourist here before?"

"A long time ago. When I was in middle school our class took a trip here. I've been back a few times, but never did the full round of tourist stops."

"I guess it's not going to happen this time either." She grabbed the newspapers and got out of the car, slamming the door behind her.

They found a booth in the corner of the restaurant, and she ordered lemonade and a turkey wrap while Austin got a beer and a burger.

When the waitress delivered the mug, she tapped the side of it. "Aren't you technically on duty or something?"

"No clue. Do you think I've done something like this particular mission before? Sleuthing is a little out of my comfort zone." He took a sip of beer through the thick foam. "Does it bother you when people drink around you?"

"Not as long as they maintain control. I hate drunks."

"I promise I'll control myself." He raised his glass. "Let's have a look at those papers again."

She picked them up from the seat next to her

and plopped them on the table. "I did notice one thing about the newspapers."

"What?" He turned the first paper around to face him.

"They're not current papers. All three are from different dates in the past couple of months."

"That's significant." He shoved his beer away and positioned the two other newspapers on either side of the first one, lining them up. His head swung from side to side as if watching a slow-moving tennis match. He flipped over the first page of the paper on his right, and then smacked the table.

"Did you see something?"

"All three of these papers—" he tapped each one with his finger "—have the same story."

"They do?" Leaning on her elbows, she hunched forward. "I guess I wasn't looking for that. What's the story?"

"They're stories about a symposium here in Boston on terrorism, or rather preventing it."

"That makes too much sense."

The waiter returned with a plate in each hand. "The burger?"

"Right here." Austin slid the papers to the side and tapped the table in front of him.

When the waiter left, Austin put his condiments on his burger and took a big bite.

"You're unbelievable." She reached across the

table and snatched one of the papers. Her gaze tripped across an article on the lower right-hand side of the page, and she read aloud. "'Leading terrorism experts and advocates for at-risk youth are meeting to discuss methods for reducing the risks of home-grown terrorism.'"

Austin held up his finger as he took another bite of his burger. He wiped his mouth, gulped some beer and then smacked his lips. "Sustenance—now I can think."

"What do you think? Sounds pretty harmless to me." She trailed her finger along the lines of the rest of the article. "Sounds like a brainstorming session on keeping disaffected youth from being attracted to terrorist organizations. Hey, I'm familiar with one of the sponsors—Boston's Kids. I did some volunteer work with that group. They do good work, nothing sinister there."

"When is the symposium?"

"This week, just a few days from now." She picked up her turkey wrap. "What was Patel's interest and why did he think Dr. Fazal would be interested?"

"Since I don't know who Patel is—yet—I can't tell you. Fazal is connected because he fingered a terrorist for us—a big fish. Maybe Patel was trying to warn Fazal about something, a warning that the guys who killed both of them don't want out there."

"About this symposium?"

"Is there a list of attendees in that article?"

"Nope." She started to reach for the next paper, and he stopped her.

"Eat." He took his own advice as another fry disappeared into his mouth, and then he grabbed the newspaper. "This article discusses security for the event, nothing about the guest list."

"And the last one?"

He slid the paper in front of him with one finger. "Bingo—a list of attendees, or at least some of them."

"Why does that matter?"

"One or more of these members might be a target."

"Do you recognize any of them?"

"A few names. One of these guys wrote a book we had to read. He knows his stuff."

"Is that what you think this is about? Do you think someone at the symposium or the whole symposium is at risk?"

"That's what it looks like to me. Why would Patel be carting these papers around with him? The information that he gave Fazal or that his killers *think* he gave Fazal must involve this symposium."

"But still nothing concrete."

"We know more than we did an hour ago, and

I have something more to report, which justifies my continued assignment."

"Why do you think Patel brought this intel to Dr. Fazal instead of contacting US intelligence?"

"Maybe Fazal was the only way he knew how to reach us."

"Then why didn't Dr. Fazal report it? Patel had been hanging around for almost a week before Fazal's murder. Nothing, right?"

"There are big chunks of the story we don't know. I'm hoping those fingerprints can give us Patel's identity, and I'm going to be reporting this latest information about the symposium. Maybe we already know something about it."

She held up her wrap. "I think you're on to something with this sustenance thing. I feel better already, and I'm not even half done."

"Finish up." He dipped the end of one fry into a puddle of ketchup. "Sustenance also includes some fresh air and a clear mind. We're going to take a stroll into Minute Man National Park and delve into a different war from the one we're fighting now—because make no mistake about it, Peter Patel launched us into battle without firing a shot."

WHEN THEY GOT back to the hotel, Sophia slipped away to the hotel shop to look for a frame but found some new pajamas instead. She needed them, anyway.

Austin spent the rest of the afternoon working, and she tried to keep busy with patient files. But she'd had enough.

She put away her laptop and bounced on the edge of the bed, watching Austin hunched over his laptop. "Did you submit the symposium presenter names, too?"

"Symposium, presenters, location, security measures. The FBI may already be working with the Boston PD on this, but I have no insight into what they're doing."

"I couldn't find a frame in the hotel shops. Do you think I'll have some time tomorrow to go out and buy a new frame for my picture?"

He glanced up. "You're not a prisoner, Sophia."

"You mean, I can walk out of this hotel any time I want and do whatever I please?"

"Not exactly." He paused, his fingers poised over the keyboard of the laptop. "Is there someplace special you want to go—other than picture-frame shopping?"

"Other than picking up where my life left off?"

Tipping the chair onto its back legs, he folded his hands behind his neck. "You can't go back to work yet, can you?"

"I have no patients, really. All of mine were Dr. Fazal's. They'll be seeing another doctor now and if they want to continue to see me as their physical therapist, we'll have to work through their new doctors."

"You're anxious to get back to your social life, your…friends. I can understand that, but you need to be careful who you contact right now. Fazal's killers could be watching people, you know."

"Oh, God, that would be awful. It's bad enough they got to Ginny." She glanced at her phone, where another message from Tyler had come through. She'd already explained about the death of her close friend. He could wait a few days. She'd even given him her cell phone number so he didn't have to keep messaging her through the Spark app.

She skimmed her fingertip over his message. She and Tyler had seemed to hit it off over coffee. Maybe once all the craziness subsided, they could reconnect. She stole a glance at Austin, back on his laptop.

Would Tyler measure up to Austin? Would any man? What other man could compete with someone who protected you from terrorists out to kidnap you? Austin would be a hard act to follow, but if she ever hoped to get into a relationship in the real world, outside of the fantasy one she was currently inhabiting with a larger-than-life navy SEAL, she'd have to get back out there and date—and Tyler would be her first.

She responded to his message that she'd be attending a memorial service for her friend on Tuesday and she had several loose ends at work to tie up, but they could reschedule their date later.

He replied immediately with a thumbs-up emoji, and she wrinkled her nose. She could never imagine that tough guy in the chair over there ever using an emoji.

Clearing her throat, she tucked one edge of her phone beneath her thigh. "Do you ever use emojis when you text? You know, those little…"

"I know what emojis are. I use them all the time when I text my nieces and nephews—even my sisters." He stopped typing and raised his eyebrows. "Why do you want to know?"

Her shoulders rose and fell. "Just wondering."

"Why do I feel like I just failed a test?" A little horn trumpeted from his laptop, and he glanced down. "Email from Ariel."

A knot tightened in her stomach. Every time Austin's superiors communicated with him brought the threat that they could be yanking him off the assignment—yanking him out of her life. She licked her lips. "What's it about? I mean, if you can tell me."

"Yes." He pumped a fist in the air. "There's a match for the fingerprints. Peter Patel is actually Waheed Jilani from the same province in Pakistan as Dr. Fazal, near Peshawar. He must've been friends with Hamid back home."

"Do they have any idea what he was doing here or why he contacted Dr. Fazal?"

"No, but the area where they're from? It's a hotbed of terrorist activity, so maybe he heard something about a plot involving the symposium in Boston." He dragged a hand through his hair and mumbled, "Oh, my God."

"What?" She launched herself from the bed and crowded in next to him to see the laptop.

He snapped the lid shut. "Waheed Jilani's eldest son was just murdered—today."

Chapter Twelve

Austin gripped the edge of the laptop. God, he hoped Sophia hadn't seen that picture of Jilani's son. What the hell had the man done to warrant that outrage?

What information could he possibly have?

Sophia doubled over and then sank to the floor at his feet. "What is going on? What did Patel have?"

"Jilani. I don't know, but it has to be something important."

"And these guys, these—" she waved her hand at his computer "—killers think I have it or know it?"

"It must be something concrete because they wouldn't know one way or the other if Jilani told Fazal anything and if Fazal told you. It has to be an object, something they're looking for and can't find—even after tossing Fazal's office."

"And my apartment."

"If we could find it, we'd remove the threat. Game over."

"God, I want this game to be over." She drew her knees to her chest and folded her arms on top of them.

He placed his hand on top of her head, the soft strands of her hair like velvet beneath his fingertips. "We're getting closer. We know Patel's true identity, and we know the information has something to do with the symposium. I've passed the information along, and at least the FBI can up the security levels surrounding the event, although…"

"There has to be more, right? It can't just be a threat to the event."

"That's what I was thinking. A simple threat is too easy. Jilani could've told Fazal or even reported it to the Boston PD." He flipped up the lid of his laptop and logged out so that there was no chance Sophia would see that picture of Jilani's son. "I'm thinking the reason he didn't go straight to US intelligence with his information is because of the threat to his family."

"It didn't work, anyway." She'd rested her forehead against her folded arms, and now her head shot up. "We have to find whatever it is he gave Dr. Fazal. We owe it to him, we owe it to Dr. Fazal and now we owe it to Jilani's family."

Austin stretched his legs in front of him and

slumped in his chair. "Are you going to try to get into the justice business?"

"If that's what you want to call it. People should have to pay for ruining other people's lives."

"Do you think your mother paid enough for ruining yours?"

"Locked away for almost twenty-five years? I suppose so. Who knows? Maybe her crime saved both of us. If she and my father had kept on like they were, she would've OD'd anyway and maybe I'd be dead, too. Foster care wasn't fun and games, but at least I'm alive."

"That's one way of looking at it." He nudged her hip with the toe of his shoe. "Are you hungry?"

"Not at all, but you don't have to tell me you are."

"I've been eyeing that room-service menu and a bottle of ibuprofen."

"Sore from your tumble on the balcony?" She rolled her shoulders. "I'm feeling it, too."

He stood up and stepped over her, reaching for the menu. "Would you like something to drink with your ibuprofen?"

"There's already hot tea in the room and a soda machine across the hall. I'm good."

"You're more than good."

"Excuse me?" She lifted one eyebrow.

"I've put you through hell since the moment I got here, and you've hit every curveball out of the park. Not sure how this would've gone down if you'd been someone different."

If Sophia had been a different woman, he'd probably be back on duty right now. Would he have fought so hard to stay on this assignment if Dr. Fazal's coworker hadn't been a black-haired stunner with hard eyes and tremulous lips?

Those lips quirked into a crooked smile.

"Something funny about that?"

"Kind of." She rose from the floor and stretched her taut body, which did a number on his blood pressure.

"You don't do well with compliments, do you?"

"It's just that I spent so much of my youth wishing I was someone else, and here you are telling me I'm just who I need to be."

"I'm sure you heard that from Hamid, as well."

"Yeah, I met him about twenty years too late. He's the father I should've had, and he's the friend I should've had for a lifetime." She touched the cracked frame.

"Do you want to buy a new frame for the picture tomorrow morning before the memorial?"

"Will we have time?"

"So far, I have nothing planned. You?"

She balanced a fist on one hip. "Is that a joke?"

"I thought maybe you needed to go back into the office, deal with more paperwork, patient referrals?"

"I do, eventually. Ginny did all the heavy lifting, calling the patients."

He picked up the phone's receiver. "I'm going to order something from room service. Are you sure you don't want something?"

"I'll make myself some hot tea later. All the excitement and the late lunch made me tired."

He pressed the button for room service and closed his eyes while the phone rang. If he was lucky, Sophia would fall asleep and he could try to forget his attraction to her for a few hours. If he was *really* lucky, she'd stay away and he could continue to drink in the way her hair kept slipping over one shoulder and the grace of her lithe body as she moved about the room.

For one amazing minute today, he'd had that body stretched out on top of his own. With her lips inches from his mouth, he hadn't even noticed the sharp pain stabbing him between the shoulder blades when he'd hit the leg of the chair on the balcony. He sure felt it now.

He ordered himself a steak, a twice-baked potato and some asparagus.

"Do you mind if I hit the shower before my

food gets here? I'm going to aim that shower spray between my shoulder blades for a little relief."

"You can always go down to the hot tub."

"As inviting as that sounds right now, I don't want to wander around the hotel—just in case. When you went out earlier, I had second thoughts."

"God, I hope they haven't followed us here. I sort of felt safe in this hotel."

"We are. They obviously know now that you're with someone who's not just a Spark date, but nobody has gotten a look at me yet. They don't know who I am, and my rental car isn't on their radar."

"My car is."

"That's why we leave it in the hotel parking lot. That's why you don't get in touch with any of your friends right now." He traced the edge of the plastic room service menu. "Maybe that's why you shouldn't attend Dr. Fazal's memorial."

She dropped the tea bag she'd been unwrapping. "Are you crazy? That's not an option."

"He'd understand. He'd understand more than anyone why you couldn't be there."

"No, no and no." She snatched up the tea bag and started twirling it around her finger. "He's family. You can do your sniper thing again to protect me, but I have to be there. I'm speaking"

"Okay. I'll think of something. Right now I'm going to take a shower. If room service shows up while I'm in the bathroom, don't open the door. Come and get me."

"There you go again. I thought we were safe here."

"You can never be too careful. You should know that by now."

"Go take your shower. I'll make my tea and watch some TV."

He grabbed a pair of sweats and a T-shirt on the way to the bathroom. He couldn't exactly lounge around in his briefs.

Once in the shower, he cranked on the faucet and turned his back to the hot water. The hotel had an adjustable showerhead, and he reached up and turned it to a pulsing spray. He rolled his shoulders under the onslaught of the water, and started soaping up his body. He was supposed to be relaxing in here, but thoughts of Sophia kept seeping into his brain, making him hard.

He dropped his sudsy washcloth and didn't bother picking it up. Instead he rinsed off with much cooler water to temper his heated thoughts.

He turned off the water and snapped a towel from the rack just outside the shower curtain. As he dried off, Sophia tapped on the door.

"Room service."

"Already?"

"You've been in there for a while. If you'd been in the tub, I would've been worried about drowning."

He cursed under his breath, dropped the towel and swept up his sweats from the back of the toilet. He dragged them on and swung open the door of the bathroom.

"Is he still there?"

"I told him to hold on." Her gaze skimmed across his bare chest and it felt it like her fingers trickling across his flesh.

He shivered. He pressed his eye to the peephole and opened the door, blocking the entrance to the room. "I'll take it in, thanks. Check?"

The room service waiter pulled a sheet of paper from the front pocket of his white coat. "Here you go, sir."

Austin signed the meal to the room and added a hefty tip for keeping the guy waiting. Then the waiter loaded up the covered dishes onto a tray and placed it in Austin's arms. He backed up into the room, kicking the door closed.

Sophia cleared off a space on the table by the window. "That looks like enough food to feed an army—or rather a team of navy SEALs."

He snorted as he placed the tray on the table. "This? Not even close."

"While you're chowing down, I'm going to

take a shower, too. Swinging from a balcony is almost as strenuous as an entire workout at the gym."

He plucked a lid from one of the dishes and waved it at her. He didn't even want to think about her in the same shower where he'd just been, naked, soaping up…thinking about her. Best just to eat his meal, pretend to work and conk out on the sofa bed.

SHE TURNED HER back on Austin and crouched beside her suitcase. As she dug through the bag, her fingers found the silky nightshirt she'd bought in the clothing store downstairs earlier that day.

Pressing the pretty but serviceable item to her chest, she sidled into the bathroom. She didn't want to come on as full-fledged sex bomb, but he might appreciate seeing her in something other than an old T-shirt, or she might appreciate him seeing her, or she might…

She slammed the bathroom door. She didn't know what she wanted. No, that wasn't true either—she wanted Austin Foley—lock, stock and rippling muscles.

She showered quickly and slipped into her new nightgown, its silky folds caressing her bare skin, heightening her sensitivity—everywhere.

After washing her face, she let down her hair and brushed it out until it had a glossy sheen.

She squared her shoulders and marched back into the bedroom, hoping to find Austin snoozing on the sofa bed and making her decision for her.

He glanced up from his plate and his eyes widened. Then he coughed and took a gulp of water from his bottle.

Suddenly self-conscious, she scurried to her suitcase and dropped her clothes on top of the mess inside. Austin hadn't even put a shirt on. He wasn't going to make this easy at all—unless he grabbed her and planted a kiss on her mouth.

Austin Foley, Wyoming cowboy, navy SEAL and all-around good guy would never do that. Making a move on a woman without politely asking first had to be against his moral cowboy code or something—especially after knowing her for a grand total of three days.

If she wanted something with Austin before he took off and disappeared from her life completely, she'd have to take the initiative—and risk rejection. Hell, it wasn't as if she hadn't encountered rejection a few...or a hundred times in her life.

"How's the steak?"

"Perfect. Do you want a bite? Of steak?"

"No, thanks."

He held up a spear of asparagus, dripping butter. "Asparagus? There's so much butter on it, it doesn't even taste healthy."

She sauntered toward him, fully aware of her nipples peaking and chafing against the material of her nightshirt—and not giving a damn.

Austin's eyes never left hers as she drew closer. When she landed in front of him, she dipped, bending her knees slightly, mouth open.

He swallowed, his Adam's apple bobbing in his throat as he placed the tip of the asparagus on her tongue.

The buttery taste flooded her mouth, and she took a bite. Raising her eyes to the ceiling, she said, "Very good, and you're right. That didn't taste like a healthy veggie at all."

He popped the stem of the asparagus in his mouth and then ran the pad of his thumb just below her bottom lip. "Butter."

"Can't take me anywhere."

"Do you want any more?"

She allowed her gaze to drop to his bare chest and wander to his flat abs. "Not…now."

He stacked his dishes on the tray with a clatter, breaking the tension between them. Who knew asparagus could be sexy?

"I'm done." He shoved the tray to the other

side of the table and stretched his arms over his head. A spasm of pain shifted across his features.

"Are you okay?"

"Still sore where that damned chair poked me in the back."

"That's my fault for landing on you."

"Better me than two stories below."

"Do you need any more ibuprofen?"

"Already took my allotment. I'll down another couple in a few hours."

"That's not helping you now." She backed up to the bed and patted the mattress. It was now or never. "You know in addition to being a physical therapist, I'm also a trained masseuse."

"Really?" He rolled his shoulders. "That must come in handy."

"It comes in handy when I jump on top of people and knock them backward into chairs. I'll give you a free session, relax your muscles and relieve some of that pain for you."

She held her breath. What if he turned her down? Would he view this as some kind of desperate attempt to keep him in Boston, keep him in her life?

His lids fell over his eyes as if in slow motion. "Sure."

She scooted off the bed. "I don't have any

massage oil, so the hotel lotion will have to do. It's all in the hands, anyway."

"I'm sure it is." He stretched out on the bed and she hurried into the bathroom.

She grabbed the little bottle of lotion from the vanity and stopped in front of the mirror to assess the stranger in front of her. Flushed cheeks and bright eyes indicated a level of excitement she hadn't felt in years. How crazy for these incredible highs coming along with the depths of despair over losing Dr. Fazal and then Ginny. Maybe hooking up with Austin was just her way of climbing out of the pit of darkness.

Whatever the reason, she had a perfect male specimen waiting for her in the other room.

She returned to the bed with the lotion pinned between her arm and body, rubbing her hands together. "I'm going to warm up my hands so I don't shock you."

He rolled his head to the side, his green eyes glittering. "Nothing you could do would shock me."

The lotion slipped from her hold and bounced on the carpet. She ducked down, allowing her hair to fall over her hot face. Where had those gentlemanly manners gone?

She popped up, lotion in hand. "Just relax.

I'm going to start with your scalp, without the lotion."

"Head on the pillow or off?"

"Let's get rid of the pillow, so you're lying flat."

He shoved the pillow to the side. "I'm all yours."

A girl could wish.

Curling her legs beneath her, she settled on the bed next to his right hip. She cracked her knuckles and rose to her knees. She dug her fingertips into his thick, short hair until they met his scalp. Then she pressed the pads of her fingers against the points behind his ears and down to the base of his skull.

He released a long breath. "That feels surprisingly good."

"You haven't had a head massage before? Even haircuts usually involve a massage when you get your hair washed."

"When I get a haircut, the navy barber doesn't exactly massage my scalp."

"Well, he should start." She finished with his head and moved down to his neck, pinching into the hard, corded muscles. "Lot of tension right here."

"Yeah, well, that's an occupational hazard. I have to hold my head in the same position for long stretches of time when I'm on a mission."

She drove her thumbs into either side of his neck, and he sucked in a breath.

"Sorry. With this much tension, there's gonna be some pain."

"Hurts so much, it feels good."

"If you say so, tough guy."

Her hands slipped to his broad shoulders, spanning the slabs of muscle beneath his smooth skin. She squeezed a puddle of lotion into her palm and rubbed her hands together. Her hands slid across his shoulders, and he seemed to melt beneath her touch, as his eyelashes fluttered and his eyes closed.

He tensed up as she worked toward his shoulder blades. "You're getting close to my injury."

"I can see it. A bruise is forming where the chair leg gouged you." She dabbled her fingertips over the red spot. "I'll work around it, and as your muscles get loose, that'll relieve some of your pain in that area."

"Go for it. I trust you."

Avoiding the bruised area of his back, she massaged his warm skin. His back formed a perfect V, tapering down to his narrow waist. The waistband of his sweats began just above the curve of his buttocks.

How far did she dare go? While he seemed to be enjoying the massage, he still hadn't made a move. In her book, this massage screamed, "Take me." Did he still have doubts that she wanted him?

Maybe he'd take the massage and reject her.

Her knuckles kneaded the area on either side of his spine on the small of his back. As she skimmed the band of his sweats, he seemed to stop breathing.

"Are you going farther?"

"D-do you want me to?"

"Oh, yeah, but not if this was supposed to be some therapeutic massage." He cranked his head around and pinned her with a gaze from beneath heavy lids. "You wanna stop, you stop, and I'll go bang my head against the wall."

A smile crept to her lips. "I don't want you sustaining any more injuries. I need you—to get me through this mess."

"Is that the only reason you need me?"

She didn't want to answer that question, didn't want to think about the variety of ways she needed Austin, so she peeled back his sweats.

His muscled backside curved into a perfect crescent, and her fingertips tingled as she ran them across his skin. He shivered beneath her touch.

She drove the heels of her hands against his tight glutes and along the sides of his hips while he moaned softly and buried his head in the crook of his arm.

After several minutes, he said in a muffled

voice, "I can honestly say that's the first time I've ever had my backside massaged."

"Does it feel good? Do you like it?"

"Do you want me to show you how much I like it?"

Before she could answer, he rolled onto his back, dragging his sweats down over his hips. His erection rose from his body, hard and hot.

She lodged her tongue in the corner of her mouth. "Looks like you enjoyed that—a lot."

"I think I need a massage here, too."

"This is going to cost you extra." She cupped one hand between his legs and closed the other around his erection, running it up and down his shaft.

Tipping back his head, he made a low sound deep in his throat. He thrust his hips forward, and she pumped him harder until he grabbed her wrist.

He growled, his voice rough around the edges. "I can do a type of massage, too."

"Really?" She widened her eyes and batted her eyelashes as heat surged through her body.

"With my tongue." He sat up suddenly and grabbed the hem of her nightshirt, yanking it over her head.

The cold air made goose bumps rush across her chest, and her nipples hardened and ached beneath Austin's hungry gaze. He encircled her waist with his hands and flipped her onto her back. He loomed above her and slid her underwear down over her thighs. With one finger, he dragged them down her legs and flicked them off her feet.

She drew her knees to her chest, but he planted one hand on each knee and spread her legs apart.

"This is your idea of a massage?"

"Oh, yeah." He crawled between her open legs, burying his head between her thighs.

The ends of his hair tickled her tummy and she stifled a giggle.

He peered up at her. "Are you laughing at my attempts at therapeutic massage?"

"I…" Her words ended in a gasp as Austin drove his tongue into her core.

He played her, bringing her to the edge of passion and then teasing her by slowing down, drawing back, leaving her gasping for more. She dug her fingers into his scalp and urged him on. Her muscles tensed as he spun her higher and higher until she was almost afraid of the inevitable crash.

His lips sucked at her flesh, pulling her into his mouth. The tingling at her toes raced up her legs and pooled between her thighs. She arched her back, offering even more of herself to Austin's talented tongue.

When he grabbed her derriere with both hands, she lost it. Her orgasm clawed through her and she opened her mouth to scream, but she couldn't muster the breath to make a sound. Something between a squeal and a whimper eked past her lips as her hips bucked wildly.

Over and over the waves of passion ripped through her body, and she thrashed her head from side to side as colored light flashed behind her eyes, which were squeezed tightly closed.

Austin, his head no longer between her thighs, pinched her nipples, extending her orgasm with shots of pleasure. As she began to descend from her high, he kissed her mouth and she wriggled beneath him, sighing against his lips.

But if she thought this was some kind of calm respite after the storm, Austin soon dispelled that notion as he drove into her.

He whispered in her ear. "Sorry, but I'm too damned hard to wait."

She felt the truth of his statement filling her up, plunging into her deeply, making her whole. Wrapping her legs around his hips, she squeezed him, holding him against her body and going along for the ride.

He stimulated her sensitive points and her passion rose again, but she'd have to wait for another orgasm because his exploded inside her.

His low growl morphed into a full-fledged howl as he threw his head back. He lifted his body, bracing his hands on either side of her shoulders as he continued to spend himself.

She ran her fingertip from his chin down his glistening chest to his hard abs and ended where their bodies connected.

His gaze pinned her with a look so hot, she almost felt the steam rising from the bed. Even though he'd already reached his climax, he continued moving against her.

"Your turn again."

Even if she hadn't been close, the smoldering way he looked at her and the unselfish way he continued to pleasure her sent her over the edge.

Her second orgasm moved through her like hot lava, and she melted beneath him. He thrust into her a few more times before lowering himself on top of her and nuzzling her neck.

"It feels so good inside you, better than I even imagined—and I imagined a lot."

"Was I too obvious with the massage ploy?"

She smoothed his hair back from his forehead with the palm of her hand.

He pressed a kiss against the pulse throbbing in her throat. "I was just waiting for a sign from you. I didn't want to take advantage of the situation."

"I knew you'd be too chivalrous to make a move."

"Enough of chivalry. I'm not done with you yet, woman." He wrapped his hands around her waist, and, still inside her, did a one-eighty so that he was flat on his back and she sat astride him.

With his fingertips, he tickled the tattoo of a rose she had imprinted above her hip bone. "At least it's not some guy's name."

She snorted. "That would indicate something more permanent than I'm willing to give."

A shadow crossed his handsome face, and she almost bit her tongue. Why'd she have to bring up her personal issues at a time like this, with a man like this?

He puffed out a breath, and then cupped her breasts in his palms, dragging his thumbs across her already aching nipples. "I knew these would fit perfectly in my hands."

"A lot of our parts fit perfectly." She folded her body forward and kissed his chin.

He jerked beneath her, his thumbs jabbing into her soft flesh.

"Ouch. What did I do?"

"Sophia, we're being watched."

Chapter Thirteen

Austin kept his gaze pinned to the glint of light on the door adjoining the connecting room. It had to be a camera.

Sophia had drawn back sharply, her knees digging into his sides, her face a mask of fear and confusion. "What are you talking about?"

He put his finger to his lips and pulled the sheet around her shoulders. Could they hear them, too? He had to assume they could.

He whispered. "Just follow my lead. Try to act naturally."

He scooted out from beneath her, rolling from the bed. He grabbed his sweats from the floor and held them in front of his crotch, although it didn't much matter at this point since whoever was watching had pretty much seen everything he had to offer. "What am I talking about? You wore me out. Let's take a shower—together this time."

"Austin?"

He turned his back to the camera lodged in the door and gave Sophia a hard stare from narrowed eyes. "You're insatiable. Shower first."

She swallowed. "Okay."

She started to slide from the bed, clutching the sheets around her, and he gave a quick shake of his head. She dropped the sheet, her body still shimmering from their lovemaking, and joined him by the side of the bed. They'd already seen everything she had to offer, too, and the thought prompted a white-hot anger to thump through his veins.

He still had to make sure that what had caught his attention was, in fact, a camera, but he didn't want to signal that he knew it was there.

Taking her by the hand, he led her to the bathroom, shielding her naked body with his as much as he could. He swung open the bathroom door and nudged her inside. Then he turned on the shower full blast.

He took her by the shoulders. "I think there's a minicamera in the door adjoining our room to the one next to ours."

Sophia covered her mouth with both hands. "What? How?"

"I don't know, but we have to get out of here."

"Do you think they're in the next room right now?"

"Not unless the senior citizens in there have gone to the dark side. I saw them earlier with family and grandkids—no way. Somehow the guys on your tail got access to the room long enough to plant a minicamera in the adjoining door. They don't have to be present, and even if I destroy it, which I will, they've been receiving their video and maybe audio on a computer somewhere."

A red stain blotched her cheeks, and she put one arm across her breasts.

"I'm sorry, Sophia."

"Oh, God." She shook her head. "What they saw us doing just now isn't important, but how'd they track us to this hotel?"

"It's not the cars. I checked those thoroughly. Nobody followed us. It can't be my phone, which is untraceable and untrackable. It has to be your cell phone."

"They're tracking my cell phone?"

"They must've been able to ping it somehow and track it down, although that must've happened recently or they would've made a move on us before this."

"I don't understand."

"There's not much more to understand at this point. We're getting out of here and you're leaving your phone…and your car."

"Where will we go? I have to attend Dr. Fazal's memorial. I told you that."

"We'll go to another hotel. I have a second set of fake identity papers, so if they got my name from this hotel, I can check in as someone else. I think we'll be okay, as long as you leave your phone here."

"I feel sick to my stomach, but I'm ready to leave now."

He pushed the hair from her face and kissed her temple. "We can't leave right now. We have to pretend we don't know the camera's there, and I don't want them to see us packing up and leaving in the middle of the night."

Her face blanched and her bottom lip trembled. "I can't, Austin. I can't spend the night in that bed with them watching me, watching us."

"Sure you can." He tugged on her soft earlobe. "I'll be right beside you. We'll pretend we're going to sleep after a lusty night of sex."

"What if they come for us at night? What if they break into the room?"

"They're not going to break into the room. That's why they set up the camera next door. I have a weapon with me, and I'll make sure they see it."

A vertical crease formed between her brows. "How are we going to disguise the fact that we're leaving? They'll see you remove the camera."

"I'm going to remove the camera from the other side. They might think it's just a malfunction."

"How will get into that room?"

"They did it, didn't they?" He pulled her close and rubbed her back, one hand resting on the curve of her backside. "I'll take care of this, Sophia. You did a great job out there—and I don't mean the sex, although that was pretty fantastic, too. You kept your cool. We'll get through this."

"What now?"

"Quick shower and off to bed."

They climbed into the tub together and rinsed off while he cursed the circumstances and the wasted opportunity of having Sophia in the shower with him.

After they patted dry and brushed their teeth, he handed her a dry towel. "You can wrap up in this if it makes you feel more comfortable. I don't think that would be unusual."

"Neither do I." She snatched the towel from him and wound it around her body.

He scooped in a deep breath and pushed open the bathroom door. He said in a loud voice, "I'm going to get my weapon. You crawl into bed and find a movie."

As Sophia walked jerkily toward the bed, Austin crouched beside his bag and removed his gun. With the weapon dangling from his hand, he strolled back to the bed, where Sophia was huddled under the covers, the remote control in her hand.

He turned off the bedside lamp and slid between the sheets next to her, glancing toward the adjoining door. The tiny camera winked back at him. He placed his weapon on the nightstand.

"Did you find anything to watch?"

She pointed at the TV with the remote. "Have you seen this one before?"

"No. Leave it on."

Sophia dropped the remote in her lap. She'd pulled the sheets up to her throat and was sitting bolt upright, her arms at her sides—a perfectly natural way to watch TV next to a man you'd just banged.

He turned up the volume and punched the pillows behind him. Sliding an arm behind her waist, he said, "Scooch down here with me."

She turned a pair of round eyes on him and crossed her hands over her chest like a virgin on her wedding night, and he knew damned well she wasn't a virgin and this was no wedding night.

He lowered his voice. "You look ridiculous sitting like that."

She huffed out a breath and slid down. He draped his arm across her shoulders and pulled her close until her head was resting on his shoulder.

"That's better." He kissed the top of her head. "Try to sleep. I got this."

She snuggled her naked body closer to him, skin to skin, flinging one arm across his midsection and hooking her leg over his thigh. His libido stirred, along with a couple of choice body parts as he gritted his teeth. He should've left her in that virgin pose.

He had the strongest urge to take her again, right here, right now—and he didn't give a damn who was watching.

THE FOLLOWING MORNING, they went about their business in the most natural way they could muster. Sophia was a trooper.

When they heard their neighbors open their door, they sprang into action and met them at the elevator.

Sophia smiled at the older couple. "Busy day today?"

"Lexington and Concord, and Walden Pond

on the way back." The woman held up a dog-eared map. "Do you know that Thoreau really wasn't roughing it at Walden Pond?"

"No, I didn't know that."

The woman's husband rolled his eyes. "Irene, nobody's interested in Thoreau."

"I know you're not." His wife tapped him with the map while she winked at Sophia.

They parted ways in the lobby, and Austin steered Sophia to the hotel restaurant. As soon as they took a seat at a table, he tapped his phone and put it beside his coffee cup. He'd set up his laptop to monitor any disturbances in the room and then transfer that data to his cell phone.

When the food arrived it could've been sandpaper, since all of his senses were on high alert, and he shoveled eggs in his mouth with one eye on his phone and the other on the entrance to the restaurant.

Fazal's killers knew they were here, and they'd use any opportunity they could to grab Sophia—because that was their current goal. They wanted to know what she knew, even if she didn't know she knew it. Thank God he didn't have to explain that one to her. She got it.

She got everything.

Sophia nibbled on the edge of her bagel. "Are

we just going to hang around all day and wait for housekeeping to show up on our floor?"

"Yep."

"Being in that room creeps me out. I can't wait to leave."

"You and me both. How do you think I liked it, walking around that room naked, knowing some guy's checking out my junk?"

Sophia choked and sprayed orange juice into his plate of eggs. "*That's* what you were thinking about?"

"Believe me, that's what any guy's gonna be thinking about."

"At least you've got junk worth checking out."

"Thanks. That just made the situation ten times more disturbing." He gave her a grin. He liked making her laugh.

When they finished breakfast, they took their coffee into the lobby, where Austin could watch the floors above and the progression of the housekeeping carts.

About an hour later, he nudged Sophia's arm. She'd picked up a paperback in the gift shop and now nodded over it.

She rubbed her eyes. "Is it time?"

"The cart's on our floor."

"I hope you know what you're doing."

"It won't take long, and the guys watching

us won't figure it out for a while, giving us a head start."

They got off the elevator on their floor and waited in the room with the ice and vending machines. When the housekeeping cart stopped in front of the room next to theirs and the maid opened the door, they slipped into the hallway.

He took Sophia's arm and pressed her shoulders against the wall outside the room. Ducking his head, he brushed his lips against her ear. "Stay here and keep watch. This won't take long."

He curled his fingers around the knife in his pocket and entered the room. With the maid in the bathroom, running water in the sink, he strode toward the door that led to his own room.

He ran his hand over the smooth wood until he felt a protrusion and circled it with his fingertip. Damn, they were good. These were no amateurs.

He stuck the point of the knife under one edge of the camera and worked it free. Pinching the small device between two fingers, he covered the lens side of the camera—the side that had been pointing into his room, recording him and Sophia in bed.

He placed it on the carpet and ground the heel of his boot against it. "Show over, assholes."

He left the mangled device on the floor for the maid to vacuum it up.

"Excuse me? I didn't think anyone was in here." The maid stood in the doorway of the bathroom with some towels in her arms and a perplexed expression on her face.

Austin pocketed his knife and withdrew his card key. He held it up. "Forgot something."

He breezed past her and out the door, squeezing past the cart. "Done. Let's get out of here."

He opened the door of their own room and flipped around the do-not-disturb sign on the handle. "How fast can you pack?"

"A matter of minutes. I've had lots of practice what with moving from one foster home to another."

"Good." He closed down his laptop and retrieved his rifle case from the closet.

Within thirty minutes, they'd packed their stuff, checked out of the hotel and were sitting in his rental. "My handlers almost booked me in a hotel near the harbor. I'd say that's a good second choice."

"That's closer to the Kennedy Library, the location of the symposium."

He entered the hotel name in the car's GPS. "I wish we had more information about what's going down there. Blind security can only do so much."

"I've been thinking about that."

"Me, too—a lot." He pulled out of the hotel's parking structure and tapped Start on the GPS.

"Boston's Kids is one of the symposium's hosts."

"You mentioned you knew about that group."

"I used to volunteer for that group. If Rick Stansfield is still the director, I might have an in."

"An in?" He hit the brakes harder than he'd planned and the car lurched at the red light.

"One of the articles mentioned a fund-raising party prior to the meetings. I think I can get us an invitation."

This time he slammed the brakes. "You're kidding, right?"

"I'm not." She tucked her hair behind one ear. "Of course, I no longer have my cell phone, but I can get Rick's number and give him a call."

"If there's going to be some kind of attack at that event, you need to be as far away from it as possible."

"Not if I can help prevent it. Do you know how devastating it would be for those organizations if there was some kind of terrorist attack at a symposium they're hosting?"

"I get it." He took her hand and toyed with her fingers. "But do you realize how devastated I'd be if something happened to you at that symposium?"

"You said it yourself. Security will be tight, and I've got the best security of all." She brought his hand to her lips and kissed his knuckles.

"I don't know if I could ever get clearance for something like this."

"I don't need clearance from the US government to attend a party hosted by an organization I've worked with in the past and for which I have an invitation."

"You may not need the go-ahead, but the security agencies overseeing this little exercise of mine are just about ready to throw in the towel on you after I told them you're insisting on attending Dr. Fazal's memorial tomorrow."

"Even better. Let them give up on me, which will free me up even further to do what I want."

"You may not have anyone to report to, but I still do."

"Then tell them you'll be attending the event as backup security. It'll be easier for you to get your weapon through, and believe me, I'd feel a whole lot better about being there if you're armed."

"I can try to do that. Call your friend when we get to the new hotel."

Once they checked in and got to the room,

Austin tossed his phone onto the bed. "Knock yourself out."

"I'm going to find him on my laptop first. Since I can't get his cell phone number from my phone, I'll have to call the organization instead."

She clicked away on her keyboard while he stretched out on the bed. Had she noticed he hadn't requested two double beds in the room? He'd barely gotten started with her last night before he discovered they were making an unintentional sex tape. Was it wrong for him to wish he could see that video? It just might get him through some long nights ahead once he'd left her.

And he'd have to leave her.

Chapter Fourteen

Sophia glanced at Austin sprawled on the bed as she brought up the website for Boston's Kids. The crease between his eyebrows concerned her. Did he think they wouldn't be able to pull it off, or did he think they wouldn't be allowed to?

She didn't know much about the military, but she did know a soldier had to follow orders. If his superiors wouldn't allow him near the gala for the symposium, Austin had to know she'd go, anyway. Was that what had him worried?

"Rick is still here." The cursor hovered over his contact information. "Can I call him from your phone?"

"Sure." He nudged the phone to the edge of the bed with his foot, and she leaned back in her chair to grab it. She entered Rick's number at the foundation and got a receptionist. They must be doing well.

"Can I speak to Rick Stansfield, please? Tell him it's Sophia Grant."

"One moment, Ms. Grant. I'll see if he's in."

She held up the phone to Austin and pushed the button on the side for the speaker, and he muted the TV.

A few seconds later, Rick's voice boomed over the phone. He never faked the hearty tone he used with the kids. Rick was the real deal. "How's my favorite volunteer? We sure miss you over here."

"I miss you guys, too. I've been busy with school."

"And the work continues. Good for you. Are you calling to join our ranks again?"

"Actually, I saw something in the paper about a symposium you're jointly sponsoring to discuss at-risk youth, and was wondering if I could buy a ticket to the gala to show my support."

"This symposium's a little different from what we usually do, since the focus is turning young people away from extremist organizations, but because of our work with kids and street gangs, we figured we'd have something to offer."

"Oh, I think you do."

"The gala is invitation only, and the tickets are a thousand apiece. I can send you an invite, but I can't waive or reduce the ticket price—even for you."

She raised her brows at Austin and he nodded.

"I'm not asking you to. If you can take care of the invitations, I'll handle the ticket price—and I need two."

"I can have two tickets waiting for you at the office tomorrow, although unfortunately, I won't be in to see you."

"That's fine. Give me the details, and I'll come by tomorrow to pick them up."

Rick gave her the name of the contact person at the office and the payment methods. "I look forward to seeing you at the gala, Sophia, and I hope you can come back to volunteer for what you're really good at—talking some sense into these girls."

"I will, Rick. Thanks." She ended the call and lobbed the phone back at Austin. "Can you clear that with someone?"

"I'll try." He reached for the phone and made his own call as he rolled off the bed and headed for the bathroom.

No listening in on speakerphone for her. As he started talking he slammed the bathroom door behind him. No listening at all.

She paced near the door a few times and heard Austin's voice, low but urgent. She gave up and fell across the bed, turning up the TV. He'd tell her what he thought she should know. He hadn't been wrong yet.

When he came out of the bathroom, she jerked her head toward him. "Well?"

"Memorial first. You'll be attending on your own."

A shiver snaked down her spine. The US spy agencies really were washing their hands of her.

"But—" he held up his index finger "—there will be personnel there on the perimeter, taking pictures and running ID's. You just won't know who or where they are, and I'll be there, just not with you."

She blew out a breath. "That's a relief. Where will you be?"

"I'm not going to tell you exactly because I don't want you looking for me, but I'll be watching the crowd—and you. I don't have to tell you not to talk to any strangers, right? A limo will take you there—one with very dark tinted windows—and pick you up right at the curb. We lucked out that the memorial is at a park, which gives us good access. While you're giving your speech, if you hear anything unusual—popping noises, blasts—hit the deck."

"Got it. And the gala?"

"We're both attending, unless something happens at the memorial. That one was harder to sell. If there's going to be an attack there, the agency isn't sure how your presence is going to change that or help. *I'm* not sure."

"I was close to Dr. Fazal. That's why you picked me out in the first place, isn't it? I didn't ask for this. You hid out in my car and ambushed me." She held up her hands. "I'm not saying it didn't work out, as I probably would've been kidnapped that night if you hadn't."

"Maybe it *will* be over at the memorial." He rubbed his chin. "For the gala, additional security will be there, and they'll pass me through with my weapon."

"Not the big huge one that hangs over your shoulder?"

"Not that one."

"Good, because that one won't go at all with your tux."

"Tux?"

"The event is formal."

He smacked his head. "Great. If I wasn't going to have enough headaches at that party, wearing a tux just sealed the deal."

"Speaking of clothes, any chance I can return to my place to pick up a dress? I didn't think I needed to pack anything formal while I was on the run."

"Buy a new dress tomorrow when I'm out

renting my tux…if nothing happens at the memorial first."

She craned her neck to peer around him at the alarm clock on the nightstand. "We probably have enough time to go out now before anything closes, so we don't have to rush tomorrow."

"You up for it?"

"This has actually been a calm day compared to all the other days since you dropped into my life."

"Sorry about that."

"Don't be sorry." She launched out of the chair. "I'm kind of an adrenaline junkie, always have been. I'm not going to wilt under pressure."

"I noticed." He planted his feet on the floor. "Do you want to look up a few places on your laptop?"

"There's a mall nearby. I'm sure you can rent a tux there, and I'm pretty sure there are a couple of major department stores where I can find a long dress for the gala. It's not going to be haute couture but I don't wear haute couture, anyway."

"And I wouldn't know haute couture if it came up and bit my backside."

Her gaze dropped to that backside as Austin bent over his suitcase. "I'm going to put on a white T-shirt, and then I'll be ready to go."

He yanked off his long-sleeved T-shirt and pulled the white one over his head. Then he buttoned a denim shirt over it. His eyes met hers. "What?"

"How many hours a day do you work out to get a body like that?"

He threw his head back and laughed. "It's part of my job. We have to be in peak physical condition for what we do."

"You are."

"Thanks… I think."

"Oh, believe me. I'm paying you a compliment."

"I'll take it." He snatched his jacket from the hook by the door and checked the pocket.

Must be checking for his gun. The guy never let his guard down—but she wasn't complaining. She just didn't know how she was going to do without her personal bodyguard when this was all over.

It took them less than fifteen minutes to get to the shopping center. As they crossed a bridge from the parking structure to the mall, she said, "I almost feel safer in a big public place like this than hiding out in a hotel room."

"We should be safe here. They're not going to expect us to be out shopping."

"Maybe I can find a new frame for my picture while we're here. I think it's just a standard five by seven."

"I'd suggest splitting up to save time, but I don't want to leave you on your own—even in a place like this."

"Let's get your tux first. Hopefully, they can get your measurements and have something ready for you by the day after tomorrow, the morning of the event. If we get my dress first, we'll have to lug it around."

"Sold."

Austin went with basic black with a black silk vest. He also rented a pair of shoes, and when the measuring was done, he told the clerk he'd pick up everything in two days.

He brushed his hands together as they walked out. "Your turn."

"Wait." She pointed ahead at a stationery and gift shop. "I can probably find a frame in there."

It took her less than ten minutes to find a frame to fit the picture of her and Dr. Fazal. If only a life could be replaced as easily.

"How are we doing on time?"

"We're fine. Most of the stores close at nine o'clock. You don't have to rush."

"It's just a dress for one night, but I'd better buy something I can wear a few more times."

"I'm buying the dress for you."

"Is that going to be a business expense, too?"

"Of course."

She didn't believe him for a minute, but she'd settle up their debts later—her debts. How did you repay a man for saving your life, for keeping you safe?

They entered the store through the women's shoe department, and Sophia snapped her fingers. "I'm going to have to get some shoes, too. Is that in the US government's spy budget?"

"It's the line item right below bullets."

When they got to the racks of long, sparkly dresses, Austin ran his fingers across one row and whistled. "Fancy."

"I'm not crazy about ribbons, bows and sequins, just something simple."

"Something red. You look good in red."

"All of a sudden you've become a fashion consultant?"

"As they say, I just know what I like. And I like you in red." He pulled her close and touched her ear with his lips. "And nothing at all."

Her cheeks burned probably as red as one of those dresses he wanted her to buy. The brightly lit department store gave his intimate comment an erotic edge, which was heightened by the devilish glint in his green eyes, as if he could undress her here and now.

She punched his arm. "Behave yourself."

She staggered into the dressing room under

the weight of several dresses and hung them up on one side of the mirror. She smoothed her hands over her face as she looked at her reflection. Usually she steered clear of bossy men—and Austin was definitely of the bossy variety.

She didn't mind it in him though. Must be because he listened to her, really listened to her, about the important stuff. She didn't even want to know what he'd said to his superiors to convince them to allow the two of them to attend the symposium gala.

Of course, those spy agencies he reported to didn't have any control over her actions, but if they'd refused to allow him to attend to protect her, maybe she would've had to give up the whole idea. Or maybe not.

She wanted an end to this madness, even if it meant an end to her relationship—or whatever she had—with Austin.

She grabbed the first red dress and undid the side zipper, stepping into it. She pulled up the strapless bodice, wriggled her hips into the rest of it and zipped it up.

Smoothing the silky material over her thighs, she adjusted the slit in the skirt to open down one leg. She stood on her tiptoes and turned from side to side. A little more body conscious than she was accustomed to wearing, but it deserved a vote.

She swept out of the dressing room, exposing a little leg and fluffing her hair behind her head. "What do you think, dahling?"

The way Austin's jaw dropped gave her a thrill. "That's it. That's the one. You look like an old-time movie siren."

She tripped and folded her arms across her décolletage. "I-is it too much?"

"Not from where I'm sitting. Let's buy it."

She left the rest of the dresses untested on the rack and Austin peeled off several bills to pay for the dress. Then he paid for a pair of heels, and her internal calculator racked up the expenses.

As they rode down the escalator, he put his hand on her back. "Do you need something for tomorrow, too?"

"The memorial? I have that covered." She hugged the plastic bag containing the frame and rested her chin on the edge of it. Dr. Fazal's death punched her in the gut all over again.

The drama surrounding his murder had been keeping her real feelings at bay. She was so busy escaping from bad guys and chasing down clues, she hadn't properly mourned Dr. Fazal—and buying a red-hot dress with a red-hot navy SEAL didn't feel proper at all.

Austin squeezed her shoulder as he steered her into the parking garage. "Are you okay?"

"I feel…guilty."

"Because you forgot your worries and pain for an hour and enjoyed yourself shopping for a pretty dress?"

"Days after Dr. Fazal's murder—and Ginny's—I'm planning to go to a party. It just seems wrong."

He popped open the trunk of the rental car and laid her dress across the carpet. Then he slammed the trunk and wedged his hip against it while he crossed his arms.

"You're not going to a party. You're putting yourself in danger by attending some function that could very well be the target of a terrorist attack. You're doing it on the off chance that you can identify someone there who might've been in contact with Dr. Fazal. You're doing it for Hamid and Ginny. You're doing it to find some measure of justice for them." He pushed off the trunk. "And you needed a dress to do it."

He opened the passenger door for her and she slipped inside the car.

When Austin got in next to her and started the car, she put her hand over his. "That was a vehement defense of plans you didn't agree with the first time around. If that's how you presented it to your commanding officers, it makes sense they relented."

He blew out a breath and gripped the steering wheel with both hands. "Let's just say I know what it's like to want justice for someone, retribution, even."

"I figured you did. One of your comrades in arms?"

"My brother, my blood brother."

"What happened?" She pressed her fingertips to her chin.

"He was a marine, deployed in Afghanistan. He was killed by a roadside IED, which was planted by a terrorist group that specifically targeted American military."

"I'm sorry, Austin." Her fingers curled around his hand. So, he'd lost a member of his perfect family. "Is that why you became a SEAL, to avenge your brother's death?"

"Tucker was younger than me. He followed me into the service."

"You wanted revenge against this one specific terrorist organization? How'd you manage that? There are so many of them now."

"It wasn't just the group I wanted. You're right. These organizations form and break apart and then morph into something else, but for me there's always one constant." His jaw tightened and a muscle ticked in the corner.

"Which is?"

"Vlad."

"Vlad? Sounds Russian."

"We don't know what he is, but he uses a Russian sniper rifle. Vlad has been around for a while. He was a sniper in Afghanistan. He moved on from that to form and lead various groups, and we don't even know where his loyalties lie. He seems intent on destabilizing the region and may have even gone global."

"I take it you didn't stop him?"

"I tried. Man, did I try, and almost faced a court martial for it. I defied orders once to go after him." Austin held his thumb and forefinger together. "I was this close."

"Then you came to your senses."

"It was that or destroy my career. I didn't think Tucker would want that." He shook his head while he started the car. "I don't get why they wouldn't let me go after him when I had the chance. Several SEALs died trying to take him down, and a sniper from our team was captured. We thought he was dead, but he escaped about two months ago. I have a score to settle with Vlad."

"Maybe that's why your superiors didn't allow you to track him down—too personal."

"Talk about personal. I can't help thinking

this whole situation with Dr. Fazal has Vlad's stamp all over it."

"Really? This is something he'd be involved in?"

"He might be involved in it because I'm involved in it."

"Does he know who you are?"

"He knows my entire sniper team, and we know him."

"Does Vlad have a name?"

"I'm sure he does, but we don't know what it is. It's impossible to get any intel on him. He's guarded and protected."

"Which brings us back to where we started— what information did Patel-slash-Jilani give to Dr. Fazal about the symposium, and where is it?"

"Two very good questions, but it feels as if I haven't eaten for a very long time and I need to answer the growling in my stomach before I can tackle those other questions. Do you mind if we pick up some fast food and bring it back to the room?"

"Whatever you want. I'm not hungry."

"Yeah, but I'm going to force you to eat something anyway. You cannot live on bagels alone."

By the time they got back to their new hotel room with a couple of bags of food, Sophia actually had an appetite and wolfed down her chicken sandwich and fries.

She bunched up her paper bag and shot it into the wastebasket. "I'm going to take a shower since I was too creeped out to take one this morning with that camera watching my every move."

"I've got an idea." He swept the rest of the trash from the table where it joined her bag. "Remember how we had to pretend showering together last night so we could talk and get away from the watching eye of the camera?"

"I remember." Butterfly wings beat in her belly.

"Remember how hard it was to just stand there in that tub, letting the water run over our bodies, keeping our hands to ourselves?"

She arched one eyebrow at him. "I remember how hard it was."

He laughed. "Now you're talkin'. We don't have to pretend tonight. I'd like to soap you up and do all the things to you I couldn't do last night."

She crooked her finger at him. "Let's shower."

And for the rest of the night, she forgot about everything except the man who'd become such a big part of her life in such a short period of time.

She even forgot she'd have to say goodbye to him.

Chapter Fifteen

The following morning, Sophia got ready for the memorial. On her way to the door, she picked up the bag with the frame. "I forgot to swap out the broken frame for the new one. I guess I'll do it when we get back."

"You need to watch out for those shards of glass." Austin held out her jacket. "At least it's not raining today."

"Are you going to follow me right over?" She grabbed her jacket and threw it over one arm.

"I told you, I'll be right behind you. The limo's going to drop you off at the curb. Stay with the other mourners as you walk down the path to the gazebo. Security will be in place to watch you—including me."

"I'll be sitting with Morgan and Anna."

"I know you'll be meeting some strangers, friends and colleagues of Fazal's, but don't go off with anyone you don't know."

"You said that before."

"I'm saying it again."

They stepped into the hallway, and he stuck beside her all the way to the front, where he hustled her into the limo. He leaned inside and kissed her hard on the mouth.

"Be careful." Then he said a few words to the driver, who must've been CIA or FBI.

When the limo pulled away from the hotel, she stretched out across the leather seat. She would be enjoying this if she weren't on her way to say her final farewell to her good friend and mentor.

He'd tried to keep her out of this, but her close relationship with him had made that impossible. For that reason, his killers believed she had access to the information Jilani had given him—but she didn't, did she?

She'd racked her brain trying to recall their last conversation and if there were any hints in his words. Unless there were hidden clues in his description of the patient who'd broken his hand in a fight, she couldn't think of anything unusual about their chat.

The park was near Walden Pond, where apparently Thoreau hadn't roughed it as much as he'd let on. That was a detail Dr. Fazal would've relished. He'd loved the area and its history.

As the car slowed, the driver got on the

speaker. "Ma'am, please wait in the car until I get the door for you. I'll let you out when I see other people heading for the gazebo."

"Thanks."

A few minutes later the car stopped, and a few more minutes after that, the driver swung open her door and helped her out as if she were a ninety-year-old dowager. She felt about ninety years old right now.

As a clutch of people surged into the park from the sidewalk, the driver gave her a nudge. "I'll be right here when the service ends. Look at my face. I'll be driving, nobody else."

As she studied his fresh, earnest face, a feather of fear brushed across her flesh. This was real.

She nodded and joined the group, waving at two of the doctors from their floor.

Chairs had been set up in the gazebo, and Sophia spotted Morgan, who waved. Sophia climbed the two steps and sat in the chair Morgan had been saving with her purse.

Morgan dabbed her eyes with a tissue. "I can't believe this is happening. Ginny's funeral is next week. The cops won't tell me anything. I'm walking around looking over my shoulder every few seconds."

"I know what you mean." Sophia flicked her

fingers in the air at Anna, who had a lost look on her face.

When she joined them, Anna spent several minutes crying on their shoulders. Wiping her nose, she plopped into the chair on the other side of Morgan. "Have the police told either of you anything about Ginny? That's just too much of a coincidence to me, even though I keep hearing Dr. Fazal shot himself."

Morgan whispered, "If he did, it's because someone made him. He'd never commit suicide."

Sophia scanned the crowd, but didn't dare look for Austin. He'd probably be up high somewhere, looking at the world through his crosshairs. The thought gave her a warm feeling.

Her gaze moved past the people standing on the outskirts of the crowd, and she did a double-take at a familiar face. Her eyes widened as Tyler Cannon raised his hand.

Her Spark date had figured out where she'd be? She waved back, a crease forming between her eyebrows. On their coffee date, she'd told Tyler all about Dr. Fazal, so he must've put two and two together when she mentioned her friend's death. Of course Dr. Fazal's murder had made the news.

Was he just paying his respects or did he hope to talk with her? She'd talk with him, but a date was out of the question—especially after the night she'd spent with Austin. She didn't know if she'd ever be able to date another man as long as she lived.

Austin had made love to her last night differently from the night before. That time had been slow and tender. The man could do it all.

As Dr. Fazal's imam began to speak, the crowd hushed. Soon he turned over the mic to Dr. Pritchard, one of Dr. Fazal's colleagues, and soon enough it was her turn.

Sophia pulled the crumpled piece of paper from her purse and approached the podium at one end of the gazebo. With her voice shaking only a little, she was able to relate to everyone how much Dr. Fazal had meant to her, how much he'd cared about his patients. She touched briefly on the reason why he'd relocated to the United States and remarked upon his bravery.

This crowd had no idea how brave.

When she finished and took her seat, the imam completed the service with some prayers and an invitation to partake of some food and drink on the other side of the gazebo.

The memorial ended and that was it. He was gone.

Sophia covered her face with both hands and sobbed as Morgan patted her back. "I'm so sorry, Sophia. Do you want to grab a bite to eat?"

"You two go. I'll join you in a minute." She dug in her purse for a tissue and wiped the mascara from beneath her eyes. Why'd she bother putting on makeup? She'd known the service would end in tears.

"Sophia? I hope you don't mind that I showed up."

She looked up into Tyler's dark eyes. "I—I'm just surprised to see you here."

"I don't want to intrude on your grief, but I felt like I almost knew Dr. Fazal from your description of him. I wasn't sure if you'd be alone, and I just thought—" he spread his hands "—you might need some company. No pressure. No date. Just a friend."

"That's so kind of you, and I apologize for skipping out on our date." She mustered a weak smile.

"I have to admit, I was crushed and felt a little foolish sitting in that bar waiting for you, especially after our first and only date. I thought we'd hit it off."

"I thought so, too."

He took her hand. "Of course, when I figured out what happened, I felt really stupid."

"How could you know? I would've assumed that you'd stood me up, too."

"Do you want to get something to eat?" He jerked his head over his shoulder. "I was back there when they were bringing the food—looks good."

"I..." She swiveled her head around. The gazebo had cleared out, but she could see people gathering on the other side. "Maybe just a bite. I really have to leave. I'm sorry. In a week or so, I'll text you. Things are crazy right now."

Crazy in that since her Spark date with Tyler, she'd fallen head over heels for a navy SEAL with a very big gun.

"Yeah, crazy." He slipped his other hand from his pocket and rested it on her thigh.

A second later, she felt a sharp pinprick on her leg. "Ouch. I think you..."

She glanced at Tyler's face, but she couldn't focus. She blinked her eyes as his features blurred into a puddle. "Whaassappening?"

Her tongue felt too thick for her mouth, and she struggled to remain upright as her bones became cooked spaghetti.

Tyler lifted her in his arms and whispered, "Sorry, Sophia. You're coming with me."

AUSTIN ADJUSTED HIS SCOPE, sweeping it across the people gathering for the food set out on the picnic tables, and then tracking back to Sophia still sitting in the gazebo. He spit into the dirt below his perch in the tree. The guys out front had been taking pictures of the mourners as they arrived and checking license plates. No guests had raised any red flags...yet.

At least Sophia had finished her speech without incident, although he hadn't been able to hear it. Now she just needed to get out of the park and head for the limo, and he'd be able to breathe.

Her friend, the nurse, got up, leaving Sophia with her face in her hands. From his lookout, he muttered, "Go with her, Sophia."

Instead a man approached her and Austin's senses clicked into high gear. He took a deep breath when he saw Sophia's reaction to him. She obviously knew him. Was that a smile?

The guy took her hand, and Austin's feelings went a few notches beyond protectiveness. She wasn't pulling away from him either. He could be anyone. Sophia hadn't talked much about her friends, but he figured she didn't have a boyfriend since she was on that dating app...and she'd slept with him twice.

Austin's heart slammed against his rib cage. Sophia's *friend* had her in his arms. She was slumped against him.

Austin did a quick survey of the grounds. The FBI guys were all out front watching people, but none of them was watching Sophia. The rest of the mourners were on the other side of the gazebo, stuffing their faces. Nobody could see Sophia—except him.

He tracked back to the gazebo, where the man had swept Sophia up in his arms. He climbed over the low railing around the gazebo with Sophia flung over his shoulder like a rag doll. He was heading toward the copse of trees—right toward his hiding place—a gun dangling at his side. Austin's trigger finger twitched.

The agents wouldn't be able to get to her fast enough if he called them in now, and he had no idea where this guy's getaway car was or how many people were waiting to receive Sophia.

He had to act now, and he had to shoot to kill. He wouldn't risk Sophia's life trying to bring this man in. He wouldn't talk, anyway.

A deep calm settled over him. He took aim. He fired.

The man stumbled and pitched backward, Sophia still in his arms. He hit the ground, and Sophia fell on top of him. With the silencer, nobody had heard the shot; nobody had noticed a thing.

As Austin jumped from the tree, his weapon slung over his back, he called in the agents from the front. He took off full speed toward the fallen man and Sophia.

When he reached them, the ground beneath

the man's head was already soaked with blood, but he nudged the gun away from his hand, anyway. Sophia had rolled from his body and lay beside him, her own head inches from the dark stain in the dirt.

He gathered her in his arms as two FBI agents came charging across the park. Austin kicked dirt at the dead man. "He drugged her. He was taking her away and had a gun on her. Get rid of him and call that limo to the other side of the park, so I can take her out of here."

The agents got on their phones immediately, and Austin moved through the trees with his gun on his back and Sophia against his chest.

As the winding road through the park came into view, Austin spotted the limo creeping at a slow pace. He emerged from the trees and waved it down. Before it even stopped, Austin had the door open.

He placed Sophia across the seat, tossed his gun on the floor and pulled the door closed, banging on the divider screen. The limo lurched forward and sped through the park.

Austin grabbed a bottle of water from the minifridge and leaned over Sophia, pulling up one eyelid. She'd been drugged, but her breathing was regular and her skin tone normal.

Scooping an arm behind her neck he hoisted

her up to a sitting position. "Sophia! Sophia, wake up."

He cracked open the bottle of water and held it to her lips, tipping some liquid into her mouth. "Drink this."

She sputtered and her lashes fluttered.

"That's right. I'm going to pour some more of this down your throat."

He tapped the bottle, releasing more water into her mouth.

She coughed and most of the water ran down her neck, but he'd gotten a response out of her.

"Keep going." He dumped some water into his palm and splashed her face.

She bolted upright and clawed at him, knocking the bottle from his hands.

"That's it. Fight your way out of this." He retrieved the bottle and sprinkled more water in her face.

"Austin?" she choked.

"That's right, babe. I'm here. You're safe." He held the bottle to her mouth again. "Drink. Can you drink some water?"

She parted her lips and this time when he poured the liquid into her mouth, she gulped it down. He opened another bottle and gave her more.

She rubbed her face, smearing her eye makeup

down her wet cheeks. "What happened? Where'd he go?"

"He drugged you. I don't know how."

She rubbed her thigh.

"He tried to take you away, but I saw him. I took care of him. He's gone."

Slumping against the seat, she closed her eyes.

Austin grabbed her shoulders and shook her gently. "Don't leave me. God, don't ever leave me again."

Chapter Sixteen

Sophia froze as Austin's fingers pinched into her flesh and his ragged words settled against her heart. He didn't mean what he'd said. She'd just given him a scare, and she didn't have to put him on the spot and let on that she'd heard his impassioned pleas.

She licked her dry lips. "More water?"

"Got it."

She wet her lips from the bottle he held for her. "What happened to him? Where is he?"

"He's dead."

She choked on the water. "Dead? Didn't the FBI want to capture and hold any suspects to get further intel?"

"I didn't have a choice."

"Did he have a weapon? I don't remember seeing a weapon, but I don't remember much after he stabbed a needle into my thigh."

"Is that how he drugged you? I didn't see him

do anything to you, but he had a gun. Who was he? Why were you talking to him? I told you not to talk to any strangers."

"He wasn't a stranger." She plucked at her black slacks where Tyler had injected the needle. "That was Tyler Cannon—the guy I'd met on Spark."

"My God. They were already targeting you before they killed Dr. Fazal. Cannon, or whoever he is, was probably going to kidnap you on the night of your date, the night they murdered Fazal. He didn't figure you'd learn about Fazal's murder until the following day—and by then they would've had you tied to a chair and under a bright light."

She winced. Austin didn't even try to sugarcoat things for her anymore. She should feel flattered.

"We should get you to an emergency room to flush that drug out of your system."

She held up a bottle of water. "I'm flushing it out. We go to the hospital and they'll ask a million questions and the doctor will be required to call the police. Low profile, remember?"

"I don't want to you suffer any ill effects."

"I'm fine, feeling better by the minute." She took another swig of water. "Speaking of the police, what's going to happen to Tyler's body back there?"

"The FBI will cover it up. Those agents will remove the body, get someone in authority at the FBI to claim national security and whisk him away to identify him."

"He obviously wasn't on their radar, or they would've ID'd him when he walked into the memorial service."

He cocked his head at her. "You *are* recovering fast."

"My wonderful Spark date probably didn't want to give me a heavy dose of whatever he was dispensing, since his bosses would be anxious to question me."

"You got that right. You slipped through their fingers again."

"With a little help from my personal navy SEAL sniper."

"Listen." He captured a loose strand of her hair and twirled it around his finger. "We're attending that gala tomorrow night, and then you're done. If nothing happens there, I'm going to turn over everything I have on this to the agency in charge and then you're finished."

She widened her eyes. "We may be finished, but what if they're not? What if they still want to come after me?"

"I'm convinced whatever they're planning will happen at this symposium. Maybe we already have the information Jilani passed on to

Dr. Fazal—and it's the fact that the symposium is the target. If we foil this attack, it should be over."

"Should be. How are you going to know for sure? The minute you leave and I go back to my new normal, they could strike."

He massaged his temples. "Let's think about that when the symposium ends. I'll let the real spies handle that."

She closed her eyes and leaned her head against the seat. He was going to turn her over to strangers. He might not ever want to leave her, but he was going to give a try.

"Are you okay?" He touched her knee. "I can have the FBI send a doctor to the hotel to check you out."

"I'm just tired."

He left his hand on her knee. "That's how they tracked you to the hotel—through Tyler Cannon and your phone."

"They knew I used Spark, too. I was such an easy mark…before you came on the scene." And she'd be one again when he left.

"Let's get through tomorrow night in one piece, and then we can think about the future."

The future? Did she even have one without Austin Foley by her side?

THE REST OF the afternoon and the evening after the memorial passed in a blur. She had more of the drug in her system than she'd thought, and Austin called in a doctor.

He'd assured her that the drug posed no danger and encouraged her to sleep it off. She didn't need any convincing, but it felt like a wasted night—having Austin with her and snoozing the time away when it was so precious.

She woke up the day of the symposium gala and fund-raiser refreshed if anxious. After the fiasco yesterday at the memorial, she didn't trust the FBI to keep her safe.

But Austin would be there—and she trusted him with her life, if not her heart.

He tapped his laptop when she came out of the bathroom after showering and dressing. "I'm sending in my report."

"Has the FBI or the CIA identified Tyler Cannon yet?"

"He's Tyler Cannon, grew up in Minneapolis, attended MIT and was working as an engineer."

"And what? Was a terrorist on the side?"

"It would appear so. He did take two trips to Pakistan in the past four years. He could've been radicalized and groomed for when they needed him—and they needed him to get to you."

"That's crazy."

"That's what this symposium is targeting, isn't it?"

"It sounds like there's a lot of work to be done." She spun her own laptop around on the table to face her. "I'm going to delete my profile on Spark right now."

"Great idea."

When she was done with that, she opened her emails for the first time in a few days. Morgan and Anna had forwarded some patient communications to her, and an orthopedic surgeon had contacted her about assisting in his office.

She drummed her fingertips on the table next to her laptop as she formulated a response in her head. It looked like she might have a job on the other side, but when would she safely get to that other side?

What if nothing happened tonight? No bomb, no active shooter, no indication that anything was over? Would Austin leave, anyway? Would the FBI leave her to fend for herself?

She and Austin worked side by side in awkward silence, as if neither one of them wanted to face what came next. All they could do was stay focused on the gala tonight.

They had a late lunch in the hotel restaurant, and Austin decided to keep it light, telling her stories about his family and the ranch. She could almost picture it—the happy family life she'd never had.

"I have an idea." He toyed with the half-eaten

fries on his plate. "If we have any reason to believe this isn't over tonight, can you take some time off?"

"I guess. I don't really have anything to take time off from since I'm already taking a break from school, although it looks like I might have an offer from another doctor's office."

"Can you delay that? I mean, if your life is in danger, getting another job is not going to do you any good."

"I suppose I'd have to. What do you have in mind?"

"My family's ranch in Wyoming."

She dropped her fork. "Are you serious?"

"Yep. My father's there. One of my brothers is there. They'd look after you…in my place. Nobody would find you at the ranch."

"I—I'm…" She pressed the water glass against her hot cheek. "Clearly speechless."

"Look, I know you're not much of a country girl, and you'd probably be bored out of your mind, but you'd be safe."

Safe and still a part of his life. Could she do it? Only if she knew he meant something more than just a duty to protect her. Maybe he wanted his family's opinion before he pursued anything with her.

"Think about it." He stuffed some fries into his mouth and checked his phone.

She'd ruined that moment. Why couldn't she jump up and down and accept his invitation with a big smile on her face? That's how she really felt.

He slipped his phone into his front pocket. "After I see you back to the room, I'm going to pick up the tux. Then I need some shut-eye before the big event."

"I don't. I feel as if I've slept for two days straight. I suppose you don't want me going outside."

"Negative. I'm sorry."

"That's okay. I've had enough excitement in the past few days to tide me over for about the next twenty years of my life."

Austin dropped her off at the hotel room, and she got back on her laptop to finish going through emails. She also took a peek at Austin's hometown, White Bluff, Wyoming. Fresh air, clean water, hunting, fishing, rodeos— basically, a world away from her own.

She heard Austin at the door, and she closed out the website and snapped her laptop shut. Leaning against the door, she peered through the peephole and opened it.

He held up his tux, wrapped in plastic. "All ready, and the jacket's roomy enough to accommodate my gun."

"Well, that's a relief."

"Everything okay here?"

"As far as I can tell."

He hung up the tux in the closet. "You know that whole Wyoming thing? Dumb idea. The FBI can probably find you a safe place, a big city where you can melt into the crowd—more your style."

"I don't know."

"It's all right." He stretched and yawned. "I'm going to hit the sack. If you want to watch TV, go ahead. I can sleep through anything."

He seemed determined not to let her speak, so she sealed her lips. Out on his own, away from this room, away from her, he'd probably realized how unrealistic it was for the two of them to make any plans.

This terrorist plot had thrown them together, they'd experienced a chemical attraction to each other and had some hot sex. That didn't make a future.

He pulled off his boots and collapsed on his stomach, fully clothed.

Her hesitation about Wyoming obviously hadn't troubled him much since his heavy breathing into the pillow told her he'd fallen asleep in a matter of minutes.

His about-face didn't stop her from sneaking another peek at White Bluff. He probably had dogs there, and she had a soft spot for dogs.

Ruffy, a mixed-breed mutt, had been the only member of any foster family she'd ever missed.

A few hours later, she took a quick shower and changed into the red dress. As she took the new shoes from the bag, she pulled out the frame, still wrapped in plastic.

It was about time she replaced that cracked frame with a new one. Dr. Fazal deserved that.

She unwrapped the frame and placed it on the credenza next to the photo of her and Dr. Fazal. She turned the broken frame over on its face and pulled the backing from the slots.

As she yanked it free, something flipped into the air and fell on the floor. She bent over and saw a small, square, black object beneath the credenza and picked it up between two fingers.

A wash of adrenaline cascaded through her system, and she spun around toward the bed. "Austin!"

He stirred, pulling the pillow over his head.

"Austin, wake up." She bounced on the bed next to him and nudged his shoulder.

"What? Is it time to go?"

"I found it. I think I found what Jilani gave Dr. Fazal and what their killers have been looking for."

Austin's eyes clicked open and he sat up. "What is it?"

She cradled the object in the palm of her hand

and held it out. "It's a minidisc. I found it in the back of the broken frame. He must've hidden it there, and then when he died in his office, he swept it off the table, maybe so they wouldn't notice it. There would be no reason for Dr. Fazal to put a disc in the frame like that. He didn't even use minidiscs. Can your laptop read it?"

"Damn right it can." He took her face in his hands and kissed her forehead. "You're a genius."

"If I'd replaced the frame earlier, we would've found it then."

"We found it now." He scrambled from the bed, wide awake now, and powered up his laptop. "There's a drive for minidiscs on the side."

She handed it to him with trembling fingers. He inserted the disc and released a breath. "Pictures."

He double-clicked on the first image, and a picture of two men popped up. Sophia didn't recognize either one of them but Austin jerked.

"Do you know them?"

"I don't know the man on the right, but the guy on left? Oh, yeah. I know him. That's Vlad."

Sophia narrowed her eyes at the man in the picture with the dark beard, dark sunglasses and a black and white kaffiyeh wrapped around his head. "I thought you didn't know who Vlad was."

"We don't have a name or background on

him, but we've seen pictures, and this—" he stabbed a finger at the screen "—is Vlad."

Austin clicked through the rest of the photos, which showed the two men obviously discussing something and Vlad handing off something to the other man, a thin, dark-haired man with an intense stare.

"These pictures are what got Dr. Fazal killed? Jilani? Ginny? Why? What's so important about a known terrorist talking to some guy?"

"Because the guy he's talking to is not a known terrorist. At least I've never seen him before." He opened an email.

"What are you doing?"

"I'm going to send these photos to the FBI, the CIA and the other agencies involved to see if they can identify him—exactly what Fazal's killers didn't want."

"I still want to go to the gala."

"Oh, we're going, all right." He sent the email and pushed out of the chair. "I'm going to get ready in record time."

Fifteen minutes later, Austin was adjusting his bow tie in the mirror with a stubble on his chin and bed head. Didn't matter. He looked just as handsome as if he'd spent hours prepping.

He checked his laptop and shook his head. "Nothing yet, but I'll keep my phone close and my gun closer."

The same limo driver from the memorial was waiting for them at the curb, and he opened the door for them after exchanging a few words with Austin.

Austin slid in next to her and touched the minifridge with the toe of his rented shoe. "I'd offer you some champagne, but we both need to keep our wits sharp tonight."

"And I don't drink."

"My mom would love that about you. She thinks my dad, brothers and I drink too much beer when we get together. She'd think you were a good influence."

"With the crappy background and the mom in prison?"

"Looking at where you are today? She'd like you even more." He took her hand. "I forgot to tell you, you look beautiful. I'm a lousy date."

"That gun strapped over your shoulder makes you the perfect date for this evening."

He squeezed her hand. "We're almost through this, Sophia. Now that the intelligence agencies have those pictures, there's no reason for these guys to pursue you. And they'll make it clear they have the photos when they start to track down the man with Vlad. Vlad and his cohorts are going to realize immediately the photos have been leaked."

"I don't understand why Dr. Fazal or even

Jilani didn't hand over the photos to the CIA right away. Do you think Jilani took the pictures?"

"I think he took them before he realized what he had. Vlad's terrorist cell may have threatened Jilani's family if he turned them over to authorities. He didn't know what to do and went to Dr. Fazal, since he already knew Hamid had connections in the intelligence community."

"But they got Jilani's son, anyway."

"They found out he had the pictures and had communicated with Fazal."

The driver buzzed down the partition. "We're about a block away. I'm going to line up with the other limos."

"Thanks, Kyle."

"What are we going to do once we're inside?"

"Watch. If you see anything suspicious or anyone suspicious, let me know. I'll alert the security personnel already in place, and we get out of there."

"Got it."

The limo crawled forward, and Kyle got out and opened the door for them.

Austin took her arm, his body vibrating with tension as they walked up the steps to the library.

They swept into the ballroom, and it seemed like a world removed from what they'd been dealing with all week. How could it all culminate here?

"Sophia, you made it." Rick strode toward her, hand outstretched.

She clasped his hand and made a half turn toward Austin, but he'd melted away into the crowd. "It's so good to see you."

"And you." He hooked his arm with hers. "I'd like to introduce you to a few of the symposium panelists, people striving to make a real difference, like you did."

She snatched a crab puff from a passing tray. Her nerves had prevented her from eating much all day, and now she felt weak and light-headed. Austin was right about staying well nourished.

She popped the puff into her mouth just as Rick led her to a group of three people.

"Sophia, this is Sylvia Fuentes and Paul..."

But she couldn't hear the names over the roaring in her ears as she met the dark gaze of the man in the pictures with Vlad.

Chapter Seventeen

Sophia had recognized him. She knew.

He knew, too.

Austin group-texted the agents stationed around the room, but cautioned them from making any sudden or obvious moves. The man whose photo had been taken with Vlad was with Rick Stansfield, Sophia's friend. He hadn't come through the front door, hadn't come through security.

They didn't know what he had on him or what he had planned.

He hoisted the .300 Win Mag, which had been waiting for him in the balcony above the room, on his shoulder, and for the first time wished he was looking at his quarry face-to-face instead of through a scope. He wanted to be by Sophia's side.

The group text lit up. No ID had been made on the man yet, but for this function he was Paul

Alnasseri, executive director of Reach Out for Redirect, an organization committed to mentoring disenfranchised youth. One of the agents had gotten hold of a program for the symposium.

Austin's heart skipped a beat as Alnasseri put his hand on Sophia's back and they broke away from the group.

He licked his dry lips, and his trigger finger itched. If Alnasseri had a bomb, he might very well have a kill switch—a button rigged up to set off the bomb even as he went down. He couldn't risk that. He wouldn't risk that.

Three agents began to move in a circle around Alnasseri and Sophia. Austin's shoulders tensed.

All they knew about him was that he had met with Vlad, a whole network of his associates had killed to keep that information from getting leaked and he was at the symposium under false pretenses and probably a false name. For the FBI, that wouldn't be enough to take him down, no questions asked.

But he wouldn't have a problem doing it. Not if it meant saving dozens of lives; not if it meant saving Sophia's life.

Alnasseri's head slowly cranked from side to side. He knew he'd been made. Even in tuxedos, the FBI agents looked like FBI agents.

A shout echoed from below and Austin watched with a clenched jaw as Alnasseri pressed a gun against Sophia's temple.

Alnasseri's voice rose. "Stay back. It's over."

Some of the people on the opposite side of the room weren't even aware of the drama, but a ripple of awareness zigzagged through the people near Alnas-seri and Sophia, and some of them started backing up. A few screamed. Several dropped to the floor.

If he set off a bomb now, there would be massive carnage. If Austin shot him dead, Alnasseri might have enough time to squeeze the trigger and kill Sophia—and there might be massive carnage, anyway.

Alnasseri started ranting and threatening, and when he mentioned the word *bomb*, chaos erupted.

Austin tightened his finger on the trigger. He had to take the shot. Sophia had to know that.

In a split second, she disappeared from his view and Austin fired. Alnasseri fell to the floor, the gun dropping from his hand.

A stampede of people headed for the exit doors, and Austin held his breath, bracing for the explosion.

None came.

Epilogue

Sophia took a deep breath of the fresh air that carried a hint of sweetness from the multicolored flowers scattering down the side of the hill, announcing spring in Wyoming. Jenny, Austin's mother, had called them Indian paintbrush, and they did resemble an impressionist's watercolor canvas. She could get used to this.

A crunch of a cowboy boot on the dirt behind her brought a smile to her lips, and the arms that wrapped around her from behind widened that smile.

Austin kissed the side of her neck. "I heard you were naming the cows. Don't do it."

She turned in his arms and cupped his stubbled jaw with one hand. "I'll stop when Maisie has her puppies and I can adopt one of my own."

"You're not going to bring the pup back to Boston and your apartment, are you?" He turned his head to kiss her palm.

"Your nephew, Kip, told me I could leave him here, and I can visit when I came back…if I'm coming back."

"What do you think?" He traced her lips with the pad of his finger. "My family loves you—almost as much as I do."

"I can't believe how they just opened their home to me, a perfect stranger."

"They're like that, and when I told them what you'd been through and what a huge help you'd been to me, it was a no-brainer for them."

"Did you tell them about Vlad? That the man responsible for Tucker's death was involved in this latest scheme?"

"I don't talk about that with them. They don't need to know the details, especially since I believe Vlad had set his sights on Dr. Fazal, anyway, because of his connection to me. Jilani handing off those photos to Fazal just gave Vlad the excuse to come at him."

"Paul Alnasseri was the perfect mole. They must've been grooming him from a very young age, and he'd completely stayed off the intelligence community's radar."

"Until the wrong guy was in the wrong place at the wrong time—to our benefit. Even Jilani probably didn't know what he had until he brought the disc to Dr. Fazal in Boston and saw the symposium lineup."

"Do you think that's when he changed his mind and asked Dr. Fazal to keep the information quiet?"

"Yes, because Vlad's associates threatened his family."

"Poor Dr. Fazal was out of it, away from the madness, and Jilani had to implicate him."

"Like I said, Sophia, I think Vlad was going to hit Fazal sooner or later."

"I'm just happy Alnasseri died before he could activate his bomb."

"And I'm happy you had the presence of mind to duck down in the chaos."

"Because I knew you had him in your crosshairs and you'd be taking the shot—whether I was standing there or not. And you have to go back to it all." She dropped her hands to clutch his jacket. "I'm going to be worried every minute of every day."

"You're going to be busy with your new job, finishing school and coming out to Wyoming to visit your puppy. There are so many ways for us to communicate, you'll probably get sick of seeing my face and hearing my voice."

"Never, Austin Foley." She stood on her tiptoes and kissed his chin.

"And when I'm done with this tour, you'll be waiting for me?"

"Where else would I be?"

"No more Spark dates?"

"Too shallow and meaningless."

"You used to thrive on shallow and meaningless."

She shoved the tips of her fingers in his back pockets. "That's before I met you."

"You take me, you get the whole bunch." He jerked his thumb over his shoulder at his family's sprawling ranch house.

"I'm counting on that." She squinted at the house. "Your nephew's waving his arms and shouting something. Shh."

Austin cocked his head. "It's the puppies. Maisie's having her pups."

"Let's go." She grabbed his hand and tugged.

"This means you're going to stop naming those cows, right?"

"Of course—except for Sydney and Clyde and Hopper and…"

He scooped her up and tossed her over his shoulder. "City girl."

* * * * *

Don't miss ALPHA BRAVO SEAL,
the next book in Carol Ericson's
RED, WHITE AND BUILT miniseries,
on sale next month wherever
Harlequin Intrigue books are sold!

Get 2 Free Books,
Plus 2 Free Gifts—
just for trying the Reader Service!

HP17R

Get 2 Free Books,
<u>Plus</u> 2 Free Gifts—
just for trying the Reader Service!

HARLEQUIN® *Romance*

Get 2 Free Books,
Plus 2 Free Gifts—
just for trying the Reader Service!

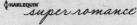

HOMETOWN HEARTS

YES! Please send me **The Hometown Hearts Collection** in Larger Print. This collection begins with 3 FREE books and 2 FREE gifts in the first shipment. Along with my 3 free books, I'll also get the next 4 books from the Hometown Hearts Collection, in LARGER PRINT, which I may either return and owe nothing, or keep for the low price of $4.99 U.S./ $5.89 CDN each plus $2.99 for shipping and handling per shipment*. If I decide to continue, about once a month for 8 months I will get 6 or 7 more books, but will only need to pay for 4. That means 2 or 3 books in every shipment will be FREE! If I decide to keep the entire collection, I'll have paid for only 32 books because 19 books are FREE! I understand that accepting the 3 free books and gifts places me under no obligation to buy anything. I can always return a shipment and cancel at any time. My free books and gifts are mine to keep no matter what I decide.

262 HCN 3432 462 HCN 3432

Name	(PLEASE PRINT)	
Address		Apt. #
City	State/Prov.	Zip/Postal Code

Signature (if under 18, a parent or guardian must sign)

Mail to the **Reader Service:**
IN U.S.A.: P.O. Box 1867, Buffalo, NY. 14240-1867
IN CANADA: P.O. Box 609, Fort Erie, Ontario L2A 5X3